LISTEN RUBEN FONTANEZ

LISTEN RUBEN FONTANEZ

by

JAY NEUGEBOREN

LONDON
VICTOR GOLLANCZ LTD
1968

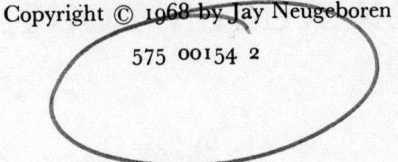

Printed in Great Britain by
Lowe & Brydone (Printers) Ltd., London

for my mother and father

LISTEN RUBEN FONTANEZ

ONE

It is too late, of course. They are expecting me by seven o'clock and it is nearly six now. So I will go. Each time I vow that I will not return, that I will telephone, that I will write a long letter explaining why these dinners cannot go on. But what excuse is adequate, after all. I am, they insist, the most important man in their lives. Well. It is probably true.

Downstairs, the men are returning from the synagogue and I wait in the hallway, watching them go by. It is Friday night and the snow which was white this morning is already filthy. I watched them this morning also, before I left for school. There were not as many then. Huddled inside their coats, they marched against the snow to the morning services, their prayer bags wedged under their arms. Every morning the same ones go by. Now and then a new man appears to pray for somebody who has just died. Every person who dies, you see, is entitled to be prayed for every day for one year. It is something, I suppose. So each morning for a year the newcomers mumble their guilt in the lower regions of the synagogue, guilty not so much for the ones dead, I would suspect, but guilty before the others, the regular worshipers. I can see the expressions on their faces, the ways they find to intimidate the newcomers: only now you come to God?

My older brothers, all six of them, they looked at me that way also. It is nothing. I did my one year's worth and that is enough, I can assure you. They loved God's laws, but it is Harry Meyers who has shoveled earth onto their six pine boxes. Not one brother lived past sixty-nine, not one died before sixty. As for me, they always said I was different and I will tell you something: in this instance I will try not to disappoint them.

A black odor, of beans and garlic, comes at me through the warm air. Overhead the chattering in Spanish rises and I hear furniture scraping, screams, objects hitting walls. Nydia and Carlos, my young lovers. Last year, when she was in junior high school, she would sneak by me on the staircase, her schoolbooks under her arm, unable to get enough of her young man. Now she is not allowed to be a regular student in the New York City schools. Not because she has a child, but because she married its father. There are rules and regulations in this world, you see. A door opens and I hear Nydia's voice move through the building. "Help me somebody! He kill my baby. Somebody — somebody! Police! Somebody got to *do* something — !" There is more crashing above me, a door slams, I hear running in the corridor behind me. Quickly I lift my keys from my pocket and fumble at my mailbox. She grabs my arm. "My husband, he gone to kill the baby," she says. "He *loco,* Mister Meyers. He flip. He pick up the baby by the legs and say he gone to throw him against the wall."

I try to smile. "What can I do?" I ask.

"You got to do *some*thing!" she says, and presses her nails into my coatsleeve. Her young Spanish face is beautiful in the shadows.

"I am an old man," I say, and shrug. I jingle my keys and the mailbox opens. There is a note inside and I recognize the writing at once. Nydia's eyes are wide. She hears the steps in the hallway behind us and runs into the street, no longer crying for help, but fleeing now, looking behind to see if her husband is close.

As Carlos opens the door I take the note from the mailbox. "You leave your hands off my wife, man," he says, and jabs a finger at me. "You call the police, I cut you up good."

"I am an old man," I say again, but he is gone before I finish, into the night, racing between cars. He wears no shirt.

I look at the note. The handwriting is the same, as is the message: my gizzard will be slit, I have had intercourse with my mother, a brother's fate will be avenged. Soon.

The note comes on an appropriate evening, I think. I close the mailbox and put the piece of paper into my pocket with the keys. Perhaps I will show it to Danny.

Outside it is quiet. The last of the worshipers goes by, an old man, limping, hunched over, supported by another. They move slowly, arm in arm, like husband and wife. One of them will be coming by alone before long. Every morning while I wait here, pressed against the brass mailboxes, they pass me, and I have never in these twelve years seen them talk to one another. Five doors east is the West Side Institutional Synagogue, where, every morning except Saturday, the men bind themselves with long black leather straps. The straps flow from inch-square black boxes, the words of God inside, on parchment. One box is on the forehead, one on the left arm, facing the heart. Seven times the straps wind around the forearm. It reminds a man that he should pray with both his heart and his mind. Brains and hearts, you see. Well. Soon the straps and boxes will be directed to new brains and new hearts, but I will not stay until that time. One day past sixty-nine is all I ask for. When they can replace all the parts, I will be in the ground. No plastic heart, no frozen brain for Harry Meyers. In me nothing is replaceable, I can assure you.

I button my overcoat and step outside. It is colder than I thought and I raise my collar so that it touches my throat. Across the street, next to the abandoned brownstones, the back of a small truck bulges with furniture. A Puerto Rican man unties ropes with his frozen fingers while his children huddle on the sidewalk, clutching their toys. I do not count them. I hear Spanish music coming from a radio and I see one of his daughters swing her hips gently from side to side. Her legs are bare. Two friends of the family struggle up the front steps, balancing a large green couch.

I pass the Park West Hospital. At the corner, the stained glass windows of the Riverside Funeral Chapel are as dark as the stone red bricks. There are no funerals on Saturday, so there will be no crowds to push through during the next twenty-four hours. I glance back at my new neighbors. The mother is rocking a baby in her arms, but its crying does not stop. Even in New York City there are not many blocks which have their own hospital, place of worship, and funeral chapel. West 76th Street between Columbus and Amsterdam avenues is not an inconvenient street to live on.

I turn left on Amsterdam Avenue and head toward 72nd Street. Negro women, their dark legs barricaded by shopping bags, wait in the entrance to Harvey's Pawnshop for the number 7 bus to return them to Harlem. The old Irish bars along the avenue are half-filled now. Across Broadway, beyond the steep rear wall of the Beacon Theater, I can see the white turrets of the Ansonia Hotel. It rises in the winter air like a concrete sand castle. White iron rails guard its aged baroque windows. Neon lights advertise the Ansonia Hot Baths, the Pels Art School.

At 73rd Street the benches which surround Verdi Square are deserted. It is too cold even for the homosexuals. In the middle of the street huge orange and yellow signs circle a manhole. Workers in silver helmets lean over the opening, cables slipping through their hands. Steam rises from under the city and I do not envy the workmen. I cross 72nd Street. Around the subway kiosk the deaf old news deliverers, bundles of papers on their shoulders, signal frantically to one another with gloved fingers. I buy tokens and descend. My glasses steam from the warmth and I undo the top buttons of my overcoat. The platform is crowded. I edge toward the front, between young men and women holding hands, and I wait. The chipped green pillars are etched with invitations, telephone numbers, political messages.

I am tired. The heavy air of the subway comforts me and all the way into Brooklyn I sleep. I wake at Franklin

Avenue. A few stations more, at Church Avenue, I get out. I make my stop at the Fanny Farmer Candy Shop on the corner and then walk the block and a half to the old wood-frame house on Martense Street. The huge oak trees leave giant shadows across the snow. Everything is still.

Inside, Mrs. Santini accepts the box of candy. Her daughter walks by, a radio pressed to her ear.

"Hi, Mister Meyers," she says, chewing gum. Her hair is in plastic curlers.

"Hello, Mary," I say. "How are you?"

She cracks her chewing gum, and I watch a smear of pink disappear at the corner of her mouth.

"Let me take your coat," Mrs. Santini says. "You must be cold. Hey Danny!" she screams, away from me. "Mister Meyers is here — come on, huh? I gotta get back into the kitchen." She shakes her head. "That guy thinks I can do a million things at once, you know?" she says to me. "It's not enough I been fixing dinner and I cleaned today cause you were coming. He expects me — "

Danny comes toward me, down the stairs, tucking in his undershirt. He is happy to see me and he shakes my hand with both of his. "How've you been? Boy, you're looking really good, Mister Meyers. Ain't he looking good, Jeannie?" he asks his wife. "I mean, every time we see you, ya seem to get younger lookin' — " He pokes me in the side with his elbow. "Getting something on the side, I bet, huh?"

"Jesus, Danny, cut it out — " his wife says. "Mister Meyers is an educated man — "

He waves at her and puts an arm around my shoulder, guiding me into the living room. "The truth, Mister

Meyers — you got a little something workin' for ya on the side? When I was in the Army, we had this old Jewish guy in my outfit — reminds me of you a little bit — he was a supply sergeant. Anyway, he was always telling me about getting nooky. Nooky — he loved that word. 'You been getting any nooky lately, Sam?' I always used to say to him." He wobbles his huge head from side to side. "What a guy he was!" He pats me on the back. "How 'bout a drink, huh, Mister Meyers? A little something to warm you up. Cold as a witch's tit outside, ain't it?"

Mary gets up from the floor, where she has been reading a magazine about movie stars. She sneers at her father.

"You heard worse, you heard worse!" Danny says as she goes by. "You and your friends — you think I'm stupid, I don't know what goes on? And where you goin' with your hair up in that crap?"

"I got a date with Joey — "

"And who says you can go? We got a guest tonight, you know. It ain't every day we get to have Mister Meyers here. You gotta remember what he done for us — "

"Joey got his car fixed up new and I promised. I'm staying for supper, what more do you want?"

"Yeah?" He considers. "Okay, then."

Mary turns the volume of her radio up and sways from the room. "And don't twitch your behind at me — " her father yells. "Remember we got company — "

"Yeah, yeah," she says, snapping her fingers to the beat.

"She's something, huh?" Danny says when his daughter is gone. "They sure grow up quick. I mean, remember when you used to come over here and she would be asleep before you even got here?" He shakes his head. "I wish she'd work more in school, though. I was thinking maybe if you get a chance you could have a talk with her sometime. She never does schoolwork unless I stand right over her." He wrinkles his brow. "You see, it's this way, Mister Meyers: I don't like the idea of seein' my daughter wind up clerking in Woolworth's or somethin' like that, you know what I mean? I figure if somebody like you talks to her, maybe she'll straighten out and get to college. You being a teacher and all. Otherwise one of these bums from around here'll be knocking her up and she'll never get nothing from life."

"I will talk to her if you wish," I say. "Though I don't think she'll care much for a teacher's advice."

"Yeah, yeah — maybe you're right. I suppose I gotta be the one to do it." He has been making drinks for us, and he hands me a glass. The outside is wet. "I would of done a better job with a boy. I mean, if she'd had an older brother, he could of helped too . . ." He makes a fist and shakes it. "Little Gil was some smart kid. He was only five and he was writing his name and adding and things. I ever tell you that?"

I nod. It is coming again. So soon this time. I drink and feel in my pocket for the note. Danny sits down next to me, leaning his body against my shoulder. "Listen," he says, whispering. "That bastard Jackson will be gettin' out of the pen in less than a year, did you know that — ?"

"No," I say.

"Sure," he says. "I been keepin' track of him through this guy in my union who knows somebody who got an in with the warden. He's been a real good boy up there — and that suits me fine." He laughs to himself. "Don't tell the wife, but I got some goodies upstairs, hid, and me and some of the guys I work with at the plant, we're gonna get that bastard good." He rubs his hands. "Gonna do to him just what he did to little Gil. We'll work him over good before we finish him off." He has his body twisted now so that his face is in front of mine, our noses almost touching. I see his teeth, broken and stained. "And I'll tell you something else — off the record — I been speaking to guys and they say that even if I get caught, given the facts — you know, going back through the whole thing, with pictures of little Gil and all the stories from the papers — they'll probably give me a light manslaughter rap and suspend the sentence." He takes his face away and smiles, benignly. "I'll tell you, though — I'd even do a year or two for a chance to do all I'm gonna do to that black bastard." He punches the cushion of the couch several times, drinks from his glass, then throws his head back, eyes closed. "Dear Christ, it turns my stomach just to think of it all, Mister Meyers — " I wonder if it is time to show him the note. "That's all I been livin' for these last few years — to get even with that guy. Make him pay." He reaches to the side of the couch and I know what is coming. The scrapbook: *Our Boy* in Gothic lettering on the cover.

He hesitates. "Ah, you don't wanna see this again, do you? It just brings back a lot of bad memories, I'll bet."

I cannot, of course, refuse him. "No," I say. "It is important for me to — " I can find no words.

He pats me on the shoulder, as if he is my father. "Later," he says. "Maybe after dinner — cause I'm sure Jeannie wants to hear the story again, the way you tell it — about finding Gil in the park and Jackson hiding there and all. And you've had a hard week with those little bastards at school, I'll bet, huh?"

I do not respond. "Sure," he says, putting the scrapbook

down on an end table. "We'll save it for later, so you only
have to tell it once. Hey Jeannie — !" he yells toward the
kitchen. "Where the hell's the grub? Mister Meyers
didn't come here just to shoot the breeze — he wants some
of that good wop cooking — " She yells back, telling him
to watch his language. He laughs. "That Gil — he was
really something — I ever tell you how he used to imitate
me? All the guys used to get a kick out of it when they'd
come over and I'd bring him out at night and give him a
little wine. 'How's your old man?' they'd ask. 'He's a dirty
wop,' Gil would say." He rubs the back of his wrist across
his eyes. "Yeah, he was something — "

I take a chocolate-covered cherry from the box which
Mrs. Santini has put on the coffee table before us. The
cream is very sweet. Mary's magazines lie in front of me.
*I Needed A Man Now But My Husband Was In The
Army.* It is a real problem, I think, and one should not
take it lightly. "You wanna go wash up — ? I better give
the wife a goose in the kitchen, or we'll be waiting here all
night," he says, rising above me.

I thank him and walk up the stairs. I hear them shout
at one another, then laugh. Pictures of baby Gil adorn
all the walls. In the upstairs hallway, above an electric
heater, Danny stands with his arm around his wartime
companions, their silver airplane behind them. Danny's
face is very soft and young. His life was before him then.
I enter the bathroom.

"Hey — how many times do I have to tell you to
knock — ?" Mary turns to me. "Oh, it's only you," she
says, and leans back toward the mirror, applying black
paint to her eyes. She wears purple slacks and a pink
brassiere which, I see when she turns and smiles at me,

has a blue silk ribbon where the two cups meet. I do not see her radio.

"I'm sorry. Excuse me — " I say, and start to leave.

"You don't gotta go," she says. "I'll be done in a minute. I can finish my hair in the bedroom. What a lousy house — only one bathroom in the whole place."

Inside my jacket, at the armpits, I feel perspiration. I glance toward her again and I see that, though she has her pale back to me, her eyes watch from the mirror. She works with a brush on her lips and sprinkles powder down her front. All the while, though, her eyes fix on me and I do not move. Her breasts are full and just before I turn my head away she shakes them gently into place.

"I'm done now," she says. "Sorry I yelled — I thought you were my old man. That guy's always spying on me." She picks up a plastic bag which contains her make-up and curlers, and comes toward me. I step to the side, but she stops in front of me. "Honest — I wanted to stay for you to eat with us. My old man's not such a bully when you're around." I would like to smile, but I know I falter. The skin around my mouth is slack. She looks back to see if she has left anything on the sink and her breasts graze my chest. I smell baby powder. "I like you, Mister Meyers," she says, and smiles. "I mean, I wish you'd come around when my folks aren't here sometime, so we can — you know — talk — "

I mumble something about her father's wish concerning her schoolwork, but the words are all wrong. She is pleased, I know, by my uneasiness. "I mean it," she says. "You're okay. Not like these high school kids or my old man's friends." She is gone at once. My shirt is sticking to my back and when I go to the sink and reach for the faucet, I almost knock over the drinking glass. The sound alarms me. Music begins again, down the hall. I relieve myself, fumbling like a child at the opening to my trousers, embarrassed at what I discover.

At the dinner table, despite Danny's urging, I leave my jacket on. Mary hardly looks my way and when she does there is nothing in her face to acknowledge what has taken place.

"Blessed Jesus, we thank you for the food we are about to eat and for all the blessings you have bestowed upon us. We ask your blessings upon this house, upon little Gil who resides with thee, and upon Mister Meyers who does so much good for us, Amen." Danny looks up. He has said it in a single breath. "Hey, pass the wine around, Jeannie — don't hog it all — give some to Mister Meyers first." He looks at me and winks. "Hope you don't mind my putting in a little word for you with our guy up there. It can't hurt, can it — even if — "

"Cut it, Danny," his wife says.

"Cut what? Mister Meyers don't mind — pass the meat-balls — I mean, if you can't be frank with a friend, what's the use?"

"Yeah, yeah — " Jean says. "My husband's a big philosopher."

"At least I use my brain for more than warming seats — " He reaches over and takes the salt shaker from in front of Mary.

"The meatballs are very good," I say, and it is the truth.

"Better not fill up — that's just the start — " Mrs. Santini says. She smiles at me. "I got your favorites for the main dish — chicken cacciatore with some gnocchi on the side."

Danny beams. "The only time I get to eat good is when you come," he says. "Chef Boyardee the rest of the time — "

"Hey," she says. "That's not — "

More swiftly than I can follow he is up and behind her chair, hugging her around the neck, squeezing her tightly. "Can't you take a joke? I'll tell you the truth, Mister Meyers, she's one hell of a good cook. I can't complain about the food around here — "

"Stop it, will you?" Mary says to her parents. *"Stop — !"*

"Look who's buttin' in — " Danny responds. "Since when ain't I allowed to do what I want with my own wife, huh?"

"Yeah, yeah," Mary says, but she looks down at her plate, picking at a meatball with her fork. Danny releases his wife and returns to his seat.

"I bet you're lookin' forward to the end of this year," he says to me. "Be rid of them animals for good, huh?"

"I suppose," I say.

"I gotta hand it to you — I said the same thing to Jeannie before you got here — you got real dedication to your work, Mister Meyers, staying in that school with all that's happening. Didn't I say so, Jeannie?"

She nods. The doorbell rings, and Mary leaves. "You want any more, Danny?" Mrs. Santini asks. "Otherwise I'll get the main dish — "

"Real good tonight, Jeannie. You outdone yourself." There is talking in the foyer. Mrs. Santini takes my plate. "You got any plans yet?"

"Plans?"

"For when you retire — I mean, do you know what you're gonna do with yourself?"

"No," I say. "No plans. I will rest, I suppose. That is all. I am entitled."

"You bet your sweet life you are," Danny says. "I figured maybe you were gonna travel — go to Europe or Israel or one of them places. You'll be getting a pretty good pension from the city, I'll bet — "

"Tell Ma I'm sorry but I gotta go right now — " Mary says, her head in the doorway. "Nice seeing you again, Mister Meyers." Her head is covered with a red and black kerchief. Brown curls frame her face. She does not even glance at me. A boy stands behind her, in the shadows, shifting his feet.

"Ain't you even gonna bring your guy in, to introduce him to Mister Meyers?" Danny asks.

"We don't have time. Sorry," she says, and is gone.

"Get back here, you — " But the door is already closed. An instant later we hear the roar of an automobile engine, the screech of tires.

"Hot pants," Danny says. "She's probably — ah, what's the difference — " He pops an olive into his mouth and leans toward me. "You get yourself on one of them cruises, Mister Meyers — take my advice. Do you a world of good to get out of this filthy city — I'd move myself if I didn't have all my savings tied up in this house — and my seniority at the plant. We got some of the coons living a block away now — and the rest'll be followin' them here pretty soon. You can count on it." He sniffs. "But you get on one of them cruises, nice and clean, with plenty of sun and good eats, movies all the time — that's the life!" He leans back. "Meet yourself some rich widow — from what I hear, those cruises are crawlin' with women lookin' for guys like you." He takes the pit from his mouth and places it carefully on the side of his plate. "You ain't over the hill by a long shot, from your looks. Hell, this guy Sam I was tellin' you about, he was getting on in years too, but it didn't stop him. When there were women around he went to town like a Jew in a junkyard — " He shakes his head from side to side. "I'll tell you, I wouldn't mind going too — we could have a good time, you and me."

I begin to laugh, but my laughter turns quickly to coughing and Danny is beside me, a glass of water at my lips. "You okay?" he asks. The room darkens. I drink. "Hey — I didn't mean nothing. That's just — "

I pat his arm, indicating that it is all right. I clear my throat. "That is a new one for me," I say. "A Jew in a junkyard — "

Danny sees that I am not offended and he is relieved. I am pleased that I make him happy. "You okay?" he asks again. He does care about me, you see, and that is no small thing.

"Yes," I say. "Yes."

He returns to his seat and begins laughing with me. "Not a bad idea, huh — gettin' on one of them cruises — you meet one of these rich old babes, you can sit pretty the rest of your life — "

Mrs. Santini brings in the main course and we eat. I drink wine now and then, and despite the talk which runs continuously from Danny's mouth, I find that I am comfortable here, at home. When I say anything, they pay attention, and that is something also. Now and then I see them glance toward the scrapbook, lying closed on the table, and I sense their eagerness. I wait. We finish the meal and I have still not begun. When I leave the table, though, I pick up the book and look at it.

No sound comes from them. There is no reason to tease.

They are entitled also. I leaf through the pages, seeing the pictures of myself, in the *Daily News,* the *Post,* the *Journal-American.* They are all here. Harry Meyers, a citizen who did his duty. Harry Meyers, a teacher and a hero. Harry Meyers, at home with the bereaved family. Harry Meyers revisits the scene of the crime. Harry Meyers confronts Jackson.

I close the book and lay it on the couch, beside me. I should not be this way, but I need time also. They move and I sense their disappointment. Mrs. Santini begins clearing the dining table. I think of my room on the fourth floor of West 76th Street. I will return soon. It has been a long week. Ruben Fontanez of class 9-15 has been playing his devil's games. Next week, though, I will catch my wild-eyed monkey. It is a promise. I lean back, tired, relaxed, strangely at peace, and briefly, before I know it, I am a boy again and I have come home from synagogue, trailing behind my brothers, hoping my father will commend me for the strength of my singing. I had put my heart into my prayers that night, I remember. My father is leaning back against the old yellow doily, crocheted by my grandmother, and pinned to the couch to catch the oils from his hair. The meal is over, the neighbors have left, my brothers surround the dinner table chanting prayers and songs, and, in another room, my father wheezes against the corner of the couch, as small, it seems to me, as I am. There are crumbs on his beard and though his eyes are closed, his head sways slightly from side to side, and his lips move. Lai lai — ditty ditty dum dum, ditty ditty dum dum. But he does not hum to the tunes which come from my brothers. My father seems very happy. The room is brown, like an old photograph of itself. The lights on the gas range flame blue and low. I climb next to my father and try to hum the song he is humming. He ruffles my hair with his hand. I am warm. His eyes open. At first he does not seem to recognize me. I cannot understand why he does not continue to hum. "Go — sing with your brothers. Leave me." He is gruff. I hum his melody for him but he twists my ear, forcing me from his couch. "Go. Leave me." My skullcap falls to the floor and I pick it up quickly and kiss it. I smell my father's feet. I crawl a few feet away, then stand up and walk around the house, trying to remember my father's melody, to seize it, but it is already too late. I open my eyes. I wonder how long it is since this scene has moved before me. Danny is speaking, and has been, I realize, for some time.

". . . I mean, the way I figure it, a man just ain't made to settle with one woman for more than, say, ten years at a time, don't you think? That's why — "

"All right," I say, beginning. "All right. I can remember it as if it were yesterday. Sarah had been dead for a year and a half, but I would still walk through the Brooklyn Botanic Gardens every Sunday, winter or summer, the way we had done all those years." Danny leans forward, intent, his eyes steady. Mrs. Santini tiptoes from the kitchen and sits across from me, wiping her hands on her apron, biting her lip. This is what they have been waiting for, and who am I to deny them their due. For, you see, I have done more, far more for them than merely save their son's life. I have not saved his life. That is more important. "My wife and I, as you know, lived on Eastern Parkway in those days, in a beautiful apartment house across from the Brooklyn Museum." My voice is full. A man can do no more for his fellow man than this, I think. I am the man who did not do what no man could do. It is difficult, then, not to join my life to theirs. "And so I repeated our walks every Sunday, revisiting all the trails and gardens we had never, I can assure you, taken for granted. As for myself, I loved the pools of goldfish most, in front of the hothouse. Sarah loved the Japanese Gardens." I wet my lips. "It was just before Christmas that Sunday and I had not come to the Gardens until late in the afternoon. It had snowed heavily and I wore galoshes. The gate to the Japanese Gardens was locked, but I knew a side trail — I believe I pointed it out to you when we went there one time — that let me in. It was a hazy day, bitter cold, and the snow had a hard crust of crystals, like a skin of ice, covering it. The trees and plants were more clear — separate — than usual that day. It is difficult to forget the sight." I pause, but they do not stir. Well. I will finish. "I walked beyond the large boathouse and around the pond, past the rock gardens. The fountain in the Meditation Gardens was frozen over. I continued up the hill on the far side of the pond, heading in the direction of the cherry tree mall. I cannot recall what I was thinking about. The snow was solid and once or twice I almost slipped down the icy trails. I remember the sound my galoshes made as they crashed through the surface of the snow to where it was soft underneath.

"And then I saw the sparrows." I open the scrapbook to the page which contains the map. It is time for that also, I suppose. I point with my finger to the spot marked by an X. "The newspapers never did have it correctly. I suppose they had their reasons. It was here — not where the X is — but here, near the grove of elms, that I halted."

I raise my arm and they follow the direction of my index finger. "You could still see the corner of the pond from the hill, frozen, and, in the distance, the roofs of the hot-houses were visible. The spot was off the regular path, behind a rolling hill. But you have been there, of course. You know." I close the scrapbook, soundlessly, and I smile. I can hear the remainder of the story, already told, but this does not diminish the very real thrill I feel again, the quickening. I am warm. I will tell you some-thing: it is not their needs only which I indulge. "May I have some water, please?" I ask.

"What — ?" Mrs. Santini asks.

"My mouth is dry — "

"Christ, move your ass, woman — " Danny says, but he does not move, or look in her direction. He remains rigid, his eyes fixed in my direction.

"Assume that the coffee table is a low hedge of bushes," I say, standing up. "And your breakfront over there the outside edge of the elm grove — the door to the foyer a vague path that cut through the trees." I pause to sip some water. "The sparrows were nibbling at the snow, there beyond the hedge, pecking at it, but there were no bread crumbs, only some vague pink spots which seemed curious to me. I thought at first that some of the more hardy Jap-anese plants were thriving — perhaps some exotic flower, the kind Sarah loved — perhaps it was defying the winter. So I moved forward, scattering the sparrows, and I saw that the pink marks were stains. I did not, I remember, even think of blood at the time. I looked up to see if some-thing had been dripping. Then there — behind the near-est tree — I saw something else." I back up, to the couch, and I continue to stare at the spot on the rug behind the coffee table. Their eyes are on it also, as if, if they looked long enough, something would materialize.

"His foot," Danny whispers. "His little foot — "

I nod, and bit by bit, question by question, he joins me in the recreation of that day. It would be too cruel to make him listen only. I do not deny him his right to relive what happened. We rediscover, then, the day, and we do so, not as you might think, by dwelling on things gory, but with tenderness and love. There are few men who have loved their sons as Danny has. We find his child together, the child the entire city had been searching for in its headlines for six days. We open the scrapbook and read again:

FIND MISSING BROOKLYN BOY SLAIN IN PARK
VICTIM, 5, IS MURDERED, BEYOND RECOGNITION
Teacher Captures Murderer

Other accounts are more vivid. They detail the pieces of the crime. They inform us that Gil was sandy-haired, blue-eyed, and nude, his underclothes frozen nearby. Laboratory tests do not disclose whether he had been attacked sexually. According to the conductor of the preliminary autopsy, Kings County Physician, I. V. Freilicher, the death itself was caused by a five-inch blade, probably an ice pick or a marlin spike.

When we have finished, and have laid little Gil to rest among flowers and editorials, tears and inquiries, it is my turn again. "I heard a crunching over there," I say, pointing toward the foyer. "I do not think I quite believed what I saw, you know. And as even the pictures in the paper show, there was something peaceful, something quite beautiful about the snow-white scene." I pause. Their heads nod in agreement. My senses are dull, but I stand up again. "The crunching seemed to wake me, and I rose and looked in the direction of the sound. Something moved. Something dark. I was frightened, I will tell you that. The snow was shadowless and the darkening day obscured shapes and forms. But I saw the points of light come from his eyes." I sigh. It is over. I can see the end. "After that it is all a blur. The results we know, but how I did it — ?" I shrug.

"No," Danny says, as he always does. "No. You — "

I put up my hand. "You would like to think I knew what I was doing then, but I cannot really say that I did. In my fear I must have picked up a rock. He — Jackson — he must have been as frightened as I was, for I do not remember that he tried to run away. He simply stood there as I approached, black and frozen, the idiot pair of blue earmuffs squeezing his face. That is all I remember. Then there were more red spots. Some incredible fury in me as I must have struck him down, and a strange, helpless look on his face as he succumbed — as if he were as puzzled at finding himself there as I was." I have moved to the entrance of the foyer and I find myself with a fist raised above my head. I move back into the living room and sit down. I drink water quickly.

"Then you ran to get the police, right?" Danny asks. He stands. He knows that I am exhausted. He helps me.

"I suppose," I say. "I really do not remember."

"And when you got back with the cop from Eastern Parkway, that dumb jig was lying there near little Gil."

"I still held the rock in my hand," I say. "And Jackson was awake, huddled in his flimsy raincoat."

"It took guts, Mister Meyers," he says. "They had to put fifteen stitches in that coon's skull. You really put it to him." He nods his head vigorously. "If not for you that guy'd probably still be on the loose, doing his sick stuff. You saved a lot of parents a lot of grief, Mister Meyers." He picks up the scrapbook and he and his wife read through it. They hold hands and he pats her gently on the shoulder and kisses her on the cheek. Mrs. Santini cries and Danny tells her not to be ashamed. She is a woman. It is natural. Even he cries sometimes when he remembers.

Then Danny stands again and curses the judge and the N.A.A.C.P. and the government. For they were too merciful with Jackson. If he had not been black, Danny claims, he would have died in the electric chair. But clever lawyers worked on the jury's guilt — all those details about Jackson's boyhood, all those psychiatrists and social workers making excuses for him, all the tales about Jackson having kept Gil in his room for three days trying to revive him. Danny has been to that room, and he is obsessed with its filth, its location. The way to take care of Bedford-Stuyvesant, he says, is with bombs. Who knows, he asks, what Jackson was doing with Gil for those three days. Who knows, dear Christ, who knows, he asks. Jackson had been following Gil for weeks, Danny claims. He is positive. There was premeditation. It was not an act done out of some temporary rage, some insane fear. He shows me pictures in the scrapbook — those from the *National Enquirer*. Could such results come from the act of an enraged man? There is evident calculation in the deed. He is certain of it. And he will not rest on this earth until Jackson pays in full. I will tell you something: I believe him.

I take the note from my pocket and glance at it. I am to pay in full also, it seems. It is late, though, and I am too tired to begin anything new. I put the note back.

"As an educated man, let me ask you something, Mister Meyers." He is intent. I think of the subway ride home. "What do you think — ?"

"About what?"

"About what he did to Gil during those three days." His voice is low, tense. "I mean, what do you think he was *really* doing in that room?"

My mind reels at the thought. If only I would divulge the best of my own fantasies, I could bring him endless joy, I know. But it is too late. If I live until sixty-nine we will need things to talk about during the remaining years. "Who knows, Danny," I say. "Who knows. Only Jackson and Gil."

"Yeah," he says, and pounds his fist. "Yeah."

Then I tell him how late it is, how tired I am, how much I enjoyed the dinner. Mrs. Santini thanks me for the candy. Danny offers to drive me home, but I decline. The subway is quicker, I tell him, and the roads will be treacherous. He curses his daughter who rides the icy highways. Mrs. Santini helps me with my overcoat. At the subway station, we wait downstairs, beside the change booth. When the train comes Danny shakes my hand in both of his and thanks me again. He puts a token in the slot for me. It is a Lexington Avenue Express and I stay awake until Nevins Street, where I change for the Seventh Avenue Line. Then I sleep.

At 42nd Street I stir. The train is as crowded as if it were noon. I smell liquor and cigarettes. The floor of the car is wet and brown, filthy from the slush on people's feet. As the train lurches forward, a young Negro, a black kerchief tied tightly around his skull, an earring in his ear, almost falls into my lap. He apologizes through glazed eyes, gold teeth. A transit policeman pushes through the crowd, pausing to look at each girl. One of them responds with her eyes and he rests his hand on the handle of his gun. I feel dizzy. At 72nd Street I rise. A young man and his girl are halfway up the steps, kissing, and we must all step around them. Upstairs there are more policemen, crowded around a drunken man, laughing at his obscenities. Verdi Square is deserted. I cross Amsterdam Avenue and pass the Telephone Company office, the Trini Restaurant, the Dori Donut Shop, where all the homosexuals have gathered. A policeman lingers in front, twirling his nightstick. At the curb, behind the green newsstand, a silver-haired man in a red convertible chatters in the cold, bargaining with a young man. A figure slouches from view. I hasten after it and grab the arm of a familiar black overcoat.

Morris looks at me, his nose dripping. "So — it's a crime, Harry?" he asks. "It's a crime for an old man to get lonesome? Leave me alone. Go to your mansion."

"Morris," I say. "Why — ?"

"You?" he asks. "You're not around young boys all day?" His eyes sparkle from the cold.

"Go home, Morris. Go home. Before you do something foolish."

"I just came for a walk — the nurse let me out." He smiles. "It's a special privilege. Forgive what I said. I just look, Harry. Believe me — "

"Of course," I say. "Go home."

"I'll see you in the park tomorrow?" he asks. "We'll talk? You'll consider?"

"All right, all right," I say. "In the park. Only go home now."

Morris gives me his blessing: I should be well and buy the bed next to his. I walk home, looking at my galoshes, avoiding stares. In my room, I undress quickly. I drink more water, I wash, I relieve myself in the hallway bathroom. I lie down. The room is black. I try not to think of the evening that has just passed. I count backwards from one hundred but it does not help and I must turn onto my stomach. It is too late to fight. Tomorrow night I will go to sleep earlier and try harder. Perhaps I will fall asleep on my back then.

It is not for comfort's sake that I work at this, you see. Here I am practical, I can assure you. Harry Meyers has been to enough hospital rooms, he has seen enough oxygen tents to know: when the heart attack comes, the man who can rest on his back has a distinct advantage.

On my stomach, I taste the sauce from the meatballs. It was Saturday night, I realize, not Friday. That is why all the neighbors had gathered in our apartment. I wonder why I confused it with Friday night. Friday night was for our family only. That is why my father could rest. I sniffed the spices from the silver *havdallah* box. I remember that also, my brothers, believe me, so do not look at me that way. I roll to my side and place the pillow half under my head, half under my chest. My nose drips slightly. I stretch my toes and listen to the sound of the radiator. I wonder if Mary is home yet. I remember her smile and I imagine her in the car with her young man. The windows are steamed. Such thoughts relax me. I sleep.

TWO

A HUSBAND, I tell myself, is entitled to his wife's extra years. The train moves out of Times Square, rocking through its dark tunnel, and in the lap of the old woman who sits next to me, I read the item in her newspaper. The average life expectancy of the American woman is now seventy-four years and seven months, of the American man, sixty-seven years and five months. I try to remember what it was then, on that walk in the Botanic Gardens when I told Sarah that if she died before she reached the average, I expected her to will me her extra years. It was only fair. According to the current United States census, she would have had twenty-two extra years to give me. It was less then. Times change, you see. "Nineteen years and seven months — I want them, Sarah. Will them to me." That was not so much to ask of a wife, of a woman who said, even at the end, even after such cruel requests, that she loved you.

Sarah, Sarah. I am sorry. I assure you I do not need nineteen years and seven months now. Two years will be enough. It is not such a foolish request, believe me. I hear a rustling sound. The woman closes her newspaper and glares at me. My lips have been moving, I realize. I smile at the woman. You predicted I would be married again within a year, Sarah, though you said it more to plague me with guilt, I suspect, than out of concern for my happiness. But that is all right also. It is difficult to intimidate Harry Meyers. I think of Danny's suggestion. Perhaps the time has come to consider such things.

At the Delancey-Essex station I get up to change for the BMT Myrtle Avenue Local. With the others, I walk past the hot pretzel stand and up the stairs. The train comes at once. In a minute we are outside. It is snowing again this morning and there will be many absences. That is just as well.

From the Williamsburg Bridge the outlines of the Brooklyn shoreline are blurred. Smoke from shipyard stacks trails through the white air. I am more tired than I wish to admit. My body aches. Tonight, I tell myself, I will leave the phone off the hook. It is the only thing I can do, unless I am prepared to talk to the police, or to endure another dinner with Danny. Three nights in a row, at four in the morning, the telephone calls have come. The voice is young, the words are the same. "I got my eye on you, Meyers — gonna doom you, man. Gonna doom you." And then the usual, the repetition of what all the notes and letters have said about my slit gizzard, the intercourse with my mother, the revenge.

"Who is this?" I ask each time, and when he tells me that I know, he is, of course, correct. It will not be long now, he promises. The notes have held little mystery. At the time of the trial, though, the brother was a mere child. I could suspect anybody, you see. If I were to begin, where would it end? So I suspect no one.

We have crossed the river. The train is pulling into the Marcy Avenue station and I hum to myself. The boards are covered with ice and the wooden platform trembles from the train's vibrations. The cold snaps at my cheeks. I see other teachers step from the train and hurry to the exits, but they do not know that I sing to myself. They do not try to talk to me and that is all right, also. Along the streets I trudge past my own students, some, I see, walking through the snow in slippers or sneakers, their bare legs exposed to the cold edges of the air. Well. It is their problem. They should have stayed home and banged on the radiators. I hum. I remember the students who sang the song years ago, in our schoolyard, an endless chain of them holding hands, weaving in and out, the words I sing to myself: *Whistle while you work, Hitler is a jerk, Mussolini is a meanie, Tojo is a jerk* . . . Two young women teachers nod to me as I cross the street. In front of the Dime Savings Bank the Chassidic Jews are already lined up, huddled in their black coats, their schoolboy's briefcases swinging at their sides, their beards warming their necks, their cheeks and ears red from the cold. I do not need to look into their eyes this morning, to have them say hello to me. Later. There will be time. I will be reimbursed properly then.

I have been walking too quickly. I breathe heavily. At the corner of Roebling and South Third, I stop. My school is before me. Junior High School Number 50, of Williamsburg. John D. Wells Junior High School, built in 1915 by the Board of Education of the City of New York,

John P. Mitchell, Mayor, where, from nine to three, Monday through Friday, September through June, Harry Meyers is a teacher of the Hebrew language. It is insane, believe me. I cross the street. I see Rafael Quinones with his *Rayshis Das* tucked under his arm and I am strangely excited. It has been this way for almost twenty years, ever since the war, yet the sight still fascinates me: monkeys in motorcycle jackets, jabbering away in bastard Spanish, pinching the behinds of their girl friends, and carrying Hebrew books under their arms.

The students shiver in the cold. The girls wait in line at the entrance, restrained by the school patrol guard. Inside, they will get free heat and soup. Across from the school, in a narrow parking lot, boys and girls shuffle in a circle. Ruben Fontanez, I know, is within. I look their way. They see me and draw their circle tighter, but this is not the time to see if they are shielding their leader. I open the iron door and feel the warm air. The tiled floor is slippery. Perhaps, I think, perhaps it has been Ruben Fontanez, my wild-eyed monkey, who has been disturbing my sleep.

In the main office the teachers complain to one another. They all agree that those who stayed home were wisest. I punch my time card and Miss Teitlebaum does so also, smiling at me. Her loose-fitting plastic raincoat cannot hide the contours of enormous breasts. She is the envy of her thirteen-year-old students. She wears a black rainhat pulled down over her hair and she looks, I realize, like a larger Mary Santini. I cannot speak. A helpless-looking young man wanders our way and Miss Teitlebaum introduces him to Mrs. Davies, the secretary in charge of assigning substitute teachers. I escape from the office. I see more unfamiliar faces walking nervously from the entrance. The monkeys will have easy prey today and, in truth, I envy them.

Let me explain: years ago things were reversed. In those days Junior High School Number 50 was Public School Number 50 and Williamsburg contained only Jews and gypsies and the Italians who lived on the other side of Broadway. Then I taught Spanish to Jewish boys and girls. Teaching was a pleasure, students were bright, I was useful. A portrait of Luis Torres hung above the blackboard: Luis Torres, a Spanish Jew, companion to Columbus, the discoverer of tobacco, the first Western man to set foot on American soil. Like the Jews of ancient Spain, my students spoke a proud Castilian dialect. King Ferdinand and Queen Isabella expelled the Jews from Spain on August 2nd, 1492. The very next day they sent Columbus on his mad journey. This was not mere coincidence, I would suggest to my students.

But the Jews of Williamsburg had their revenge. In 1934 the parents drove the language of the Inquisition from the school. They attacked the Board of Education with petitions, demanding that Hebrew — a useful and traditional language, they said — be placed in the curriculum. The outcome was never in doubt. Harry Meyers surrendered with the Board of Education. When the expulsion from the Spanish classes took place, he became a teacher of Hebrew. It was not such a difficult thing to do. I knew the language. There were emergency examinations at Livingston Street. Sarah and I did not have to disrupt our lives. It was no small thing at the time, believe me.

I have remained here since then, through all transitions. For just as the Moors had followed the Jews from Africa to Spain, so the colored followed them to Williamsburg.

The war came, Jews prospered, and those who could afford it left the area. The city built projects for the black newcomers, and when, in time, they too began to leave the neighborhood, the monkeys climbed into the evacuated buildings. Hebrew remained in the curriculum. Who was left to organize petitions, after all. Not monkeys, I can assure you. As for Harry Meyers, his chance to get out had passed long before. He does not fool himself about such things.

Along the hallways, I see signs which promise a life without poverty. Above the students' cafeteria is a huge poster: *"Los últimos serán los primeros."* Nobody is fooled. Here students do not look at pictures and posters. Remove all signs and replace them with mirrors. Then the children will pay attention. I walk back up the stairs and lock my galoshes and overcoat in the closet of my official room. I sip the tea I have purchased in the teacher's cafeteria and look out over the empty rows of desks and chairs, engraved with the names and obscenities of generations of students, Spanish carvings obscuring Jewish and Negro curses.

I will tell you something: it will be as quiet when they are in their seats as it is now. When Harry Meyers enters a classroom there is silence. When I ask a question, hands go up. When I assign homework, it is done. The other teachers marvel at me. Their tales of fights, of knifings, of foul language, of ignorance: they are nothing to me. "In my classes," I tell them, "the Inquisition reigns." They do not understand, though. They try still to love their children, to help them, to offer futures. They get nowhere.

I crumple the plastic cup and drop it into my wastebasket. I take out my Hebrew books. Monkeys are monkeys, you see. Anybody can tame them. Here Harry Meyers rules, it is true, but elsewhere things are different. In the back compartment of my briefcase are the other books. I leave them where they are and zip my briefcase closed. I place it on the floor, under the desk, and go to the window. I do not look at the students below. I do not look at the buildings across the street. I think only of my other students.

I am also, you see, still a teacher of Spanish. For almost thirteen years now, I have held the other job, and even Morris's arguments cannot persuade me to give it up. When Harry Meyers retires he will be able to take care of himself. There will be no nursing homes, no city hospitals, no charity. I will have money accumulated, I will account to nobody.

I hear the first buzzer, and I return to my desk. Beyond my classroom the noises begin. It is nothing. I think of three o'clock. That is when I will take my briefcase and walk away from the school, past the Brooklyn-Queens Expressway, beyond Broadway, to Cuomo Street, where I am employed by a Chassidic Yeshiva to teach Spanish to their madmen. Well. Do not let their long black coats and their holy beards fool you. They are all madmen, especially the young ones. Look into their eyes sometime and you will see that it is true.

I hear my monkeys outside my room, running through the hallways. I hear the shouts of teachers and I rise from my desk and go to the door. I open it and look out. When they see Harry Meyers, students stop running. Their transistor radios are turned off. As they pass my classroom, their eyes scan the floor. My own students walk quietly to their seats. They take out their books. At once the monitors are at work: the blackboard is washed, the coat closet opened, the attendance taken. I close the door and walk the aisles. My students work.

There was another note in my mailbox this morning, I remember, but I think only of the end of the day, of the cowboys who lie in wait for me. All weekend long, Morris has been warning me. They terrify him. When we were boys it was different. Then we invented the term to mock them. We would wait outside the Chassidic Yeshiva and as they shuffled down the streets away from us, their long silken coats sweeping the gutters, their eyes fixed downward under their broad-brimmed black hats, we hurled our taunts at them. We were boys as they were, Jews as they were, but Americans as they were not.

The Chassidic Jews of the eastern European villages, my father told me, would greet their Rebbes by riding backwards on horses. The Belzer Chassidim, whose descendants were packed together in a corner of our neighborhood, wore their shirts unbuttoned even in winter. Their hearts were exposed to the Lord. They believed in the transmigration of souls, we discovered, and so we would yell after them that in their next incarnation they would not even be cowboys. They would be the rocks and the grass which receive the leavings of cows.

Now, though, Morris is frightened. Times change, you see. Every morning he prays for my safety. There is no reasoning with him anymore. He is an old man. He fears "the evil eye," the somersaults they turn when they worship, the power of their Ba'al Shem Tov. As for me, I try to make light of his fears and, in truth, I think of only one thing now: the end of the year. Then I will retire, I will cease my ridiculous odyssey. I will leave my monkeys and cowboys.

My monkeys have stopped bothering me long ago.

B*

With my cowboys, though, there is something new every day — a dead bird in my desk, parts of animals in my locker, unsigned notes which predict gruesome future incarnations. I teach an evil language, they say. I am a victim of Satan's Chassidism. My own arguments prove useless. They submit only to serve the Lord with greater joy. Perhaps it is so. Years ago, when the position of Spanish teacher at their Yeshiva became available, the other Yeshivas accused them of being renegades. But my cowboys knew what they were doing. I had been hired to train their young men in the language needed to deal in rents, in loans, in the sale of jewels. To their clients they claim to be, not from the *shtetls* of Galicia, but from the cellars of the Marranos. They are the descendants of the Spanish Jews who, after 1492, took their religion underground. They too know of Luis Torres, though the knowledge has not passed to them from my lips.

In the aisle next to the window, the third seat from the front is deserted. Ruben Fontanez is somewhere else this morning. Well. There are other things to think about. Morris presses me to move in with him, to use my Board of Education pension to buy the bed next to his. Prices are rising. What will my savings be worth in a few years, he asks. Now I can afford the price of a lifetime bed. Later they will suck blood from me. The administrators of his home read newspapers also, I think. They depend on statistics. For every man who reaches seventy-five, seven men leave empty beds at sixty-six.

There is laughter and my eyes shift to the door. Other eyes look back at me through the window, then are gone. Hector Cruz giggles. Maria Sanabria makes noises in her mouth. I pull the door open, but the corridor is empty. I place the knuckles of my right hand on Hector's head. The class is still. I think of Menachem Schiffenbauer, the Rebbe's son, at work on a new translation of the *Zohar*, from Spanish to Hebrew. William Wright, one of my Negro students, presses a hand on his mouth to stifle a giggle. I could clamp my fingers on the nerves at the back of his neck, but I leave him alone. It is best if I save my energy. At three-thirty I will need it.

I step into the corridor and walk to the boys' bathroom. A frail misshapen monkey scurries by me. It is Manuel Alvarez, from the C.R.M.D. class. Above the urinals obscene drawings and swastikas mingle with warnings, in Spanish, of the girls who have the sickness. I wander past Manuel's room, where the students are already at work, shining teacher's shoes, playing knock-hockey, watching their television shows. Manuel crouches in a corner of the room, a pygmy of a monkey. His eyelids droop, his mouth hangs open, but I wonder. There is something about him that makes me think he is more than a child with retarded mental development. It is a thought I do not dwell upon. I return to my own room and close the door behind me.

You must understand something: I was not always like this. When the monkeys first began trickling into the school, Harry Meyers tried to be kind to them. Perhaps it was Sarah's influence. They are a strange people in a strange land, she said. She spoke to me of the war which had just passed, and I was not without feeling. Give them time, Harry. Give them time, she said. So I tried. Believe me. I helped them, I tutored, I was easy in discipline, I brought them home for warm dinners. It got me nowhere. They exhausted me. They did to me what they do to the others. And so I began to find weapons.

I did so out of necessity, I assure you, though not without some pleasure. When I squeezed a monkey on the muscle of his arm, I discovered that he would listen to me. I found other spots: the back of the neck, the shoulder muscles, the ears. The correct pressure wrought wonders. Sarah reminded me that half of them did not know their rightful fathers, that they would wait turns in the winter to use the shoes which allowed them to play outside: but the conditions of their life were nothing to me. Around the school I became known as Mad-Man Meyers. My reputation grew. Sarah never knew and that is just as well. The Jewish students, the Negroes, the Italians — if you laid a hand on them you would have rabbis and mothers and priests counseling with the principal. Monkeys told no tales. Your ghost has haunted me from time to time, Sarah. I admit it. But I have stayed alive. It is no small thing.

At the buzzer, I give the order and my students line up at the side of the room. I open the door and they march in pairs down the corridor. Danny would be proud, I think, if he knew of my methods, my reputation.

My students, of course, know of Danny. A glass-enclosed bulletin board on the second floor tells them the story. The articles and pictures have been there for more than twelve years and have played no small part in maintaining my reputation. I admit it. My first class of the day files into the room and I tell them to take out their books and begin the exercises in their workbooks, at the back of chapter six: *Jacob and Leah on the Kibbutz.* I walk the aisles and examine their work. I will tell you something: they are not idiots. Monkeys who have studied with Harry Meyers can recite the *Aleph-Bes* and translate from the Hebrew language. In my classes students learn a subject. I am not in the business of vocational training.

I bend over, aware of how the points of Gladys Yambo's lavender sweater hypnotize the boys who sit around her. She writes her answers in Hebrew and I correct her lettering. I glare at the others and they are quick to fix their eyes on their own work. "You are improving, Gladys," I say, and walk on. It will be a long day, and though I still take some small pleasure in the fact that I teach something, the joy which once accompanied my exercise of authority, I know, has long since disappeared. There is no danger in my actions, no cleverness in their resistance.

Only Ruben Fontanez threatens to change things. Ah, Ruben, Ruben. We do not fool one another, do we. The first time I saw you, less than eight weeks ago, when the school clerk brought you to me to enroll you in my official class, I knew you meant trouble in my life. But that is all right also. I am ready.

I sit in front of the room and call the students to me, one at a time, to check their homework. I think of Ruben Fontanez. He seemed, at first glance, to be like the others, an ordinary monkey. He was a little shorter than most, perhaps a little uglier. A bump rose from the left side of his forehead. His mouth, his nose, and his eyes were pinched together in the center of his face. His face was the face of a monkey, it is true, but his eyes, you see, his eyes were the eyes of a cowboy.

There is nothing to do but wait. I grade my students' homework and wonder why they should fear Harry Meyers. I was not so different, my brothers. Sarah understood what it meant to be the last of seven boys. I was not born to change anything. It is enough for the youngest to survive. I look into my students' faces and, where the empty seat is, I can see Ruben, his neck craned forward, his lopsided head lowered toward his desk, his eyes upon me. Lately, when he is present, the others are bolder. They laugh when my back is turned, they answer questions without raising their hands. Ruben says nothing. Before and after class I see them cluster around him. With him, my threats and weapons are useless. Harry, Harry, you are an old man. Hurry from the school.

Soon, I reply. Soon. But where, I wonder, is my wild-eyed monkey. Despite his absence from official class this morning, I am certain he is in the building. I feel his eyes. He knows, you see. I have seen him between classes, next to the biology laboratory, his eyes poring over the bulletin board that I myself have lingered over more often than I care to admit. Not the one that secures my reputation, but another. One time I pressed my fingers into the muscle that joins his shoulder to his neck, forcing him to move on, but he seemed to feel no pain. "I seen you too," he said, and smiled. They are the only words I have ever heard from him.

Still, there should be nothing strange here. Millions of Americans, I am certain, have read the same magazine articles. It is natural for a young boy to be fascinated by the future. I have seen other students in front of the board, taking notes, astounded by the miracles of coming decades, by spare parts and transplants and organ banks, by fetal surgery and cold storage embryos.

On the Frontiers of Medicine: Control of Life. When the buzzer sounds, I send José Colon back to his seat. I collect the work they have done this period. The halls swell with noise. In my room new monkeys replace the ones who have left. In my thoughts, Ruben remains. I cannot fool myself. He has seen the full-color picture of a completely rebuilt person, made solely of synthetic and transplanted parts, of Dacron arteries and silicone rubber lungs. The captions are irrelevant. Ruben knows. It is only a question of time.

The day passes. Outside, the snow ceases to drop from the sky and the sun appears. In the street below, the old men sit on the stoops, waiting for the dismissal bell. Then they will get a chance to observe the young Spanish girls. The ice turns to water, the snow to slush. I pull down the shades to keep the sun out. At lunchtime I buy a cheese sandwich in the teachers' cafeteria and retire to the teachers' lounge. Mr. Greenfeld, the C.R.M.D. teacher, is asleep on the couch. At night he moonlights as a bartender. He places the bets on football and basketball games for the other teachers. His class goes unattended. His weapons are equal to mine. On the first day of the semester he informs his class that he is a former marine. He locks the door, pulls the shades, and beats up the strongest boy in his class. If he has trouble the second day, he orders the strongest boy to beat up the troublemaker. By the third day of each semester his job is secure.

Across the street, in a third-story window, a Puerto Rican woman suckles her child. A substitute teacher stares at her. She laughs and blows him a kiss. He looks at me. I do not respond. He turns and leaves the room, flustered. It is too late, I think. Nothing that *Life* magazine predicts will come to pass for Harry Meyers. This body will leave the way it came. There is little danger for anyone. There will be no superior race bred in test tubes, no facsimiles of great men reproduced from single cell tissue-cultures. I have nothing to fear, I remind myself. I wonder, though, if I am the only one who sees it. Perhaps Ruben is already plotting with the cowboys. When the first silicone hearts are ready and the pumps are primed, you see, when they have put the first brains into cold storage, then the monkeys will invade. They are waiting.

The thought amuses me. Ruben and his monkeys will storm the walls of the hospitals and the laboratories and the organ banks. The cowboys and the colored will ride with him. The police will be powerless. Some things people will accept, but no man will ever carry a new heart while others are asked to wait. Of this I am certain.

I put the crusts of rye bread into the cellophane sandwich bag and drop it in the wastebasket. You are playing games, Harry Meyers, I tell myself. Enough. Mr. Greenfeld turns in his sleep and begins to snore. I sip my tea. Perhaps Morris is right. The cowboys will drive me mad. Perhaps Ruben knows nothing. He is only a boy, after all.

I am feeling better. Some of the aching has left my body. I think of the story in the article, of the dead man's family who donated his kidney so that another man might live. I can see the pictures of the doctors rushing the dead man's kidney to the hospital in a bucket, grafting it into the waiting patient. *Gift Of Life From The Dead*. The living man's excretory functions were restored. I see him and his wife as they smile at me. I wonder if they get together for dinner with the family of the man whose kidney they use.

Mr. Greenfeld rubs his eyes. The steam pipe in the corner of the room knocks. I am warm. I close my eyes. Why should I fear Ruben when there are phone calls and cowboys to worry about. I will be retired before Jackson is released. That is something. My brother Simon can rest in peace then. It was a sin against God that Harry Meyers should be a teacher of His language. All my other transgressions he forgave.

May you rest in peace, Simon, wherever you are. If you hold a grudge, I do not blame you. The room is too warm. "You are the only one left, Harry. Answer me the truth: will you pray for me? I have no sons left. All our brothers are gone." I hear his voice. I am in the hospital room and it smells of ammonia. I stand by the bed, petrified by the face before me, freshly shaven, soft and pink. I looked more like Simon than any of the others, people said. He was second youngest. You could tell we were brothers. The blood leaks down from its perch beside his bed, the tubes run from his nose, the other relatives shake their heads. This body once pounded my body, I remember, when it caught me raiding the icebox on Yom Kippur. Simon Meyers, good enough, some said, to be a champion like Benny Leonard. Eighteen hours of fasting had only made him stronger. Did you hate me all those years, Simon? Our lives went their separate ways, we were brothers at weddings and funerals only. When our father died I went to the synagogue every morning for a year. You knew.

"One year is enough, Simon. I am sorry."

There was no need for that, Harry. He had wanted you to lie to him. He would not have questioned you if you had said yes. That was foolish. He had seen his own two sons in the grave before him. Simon, Simon. It seems impossible to me that you were only sixteen years old when you caught me. You won the middleweight tournament at the Educational Alliance. People had plans for you. You were only four years older than me. This spring you would be sixty-nine. You were no champion. Less than two years ago I covered you with dirt. You spent your

life like our father and our brothers, candling eggs in
the semi-darkness behind a drawn curtain. In the old
warehouse near the 18th Street pier: *Meyers Butter &
Eggs.* I could have said yes, I suppose, since you were the
last. I wonder: do you remember that night you chased me
around the house and I hid from you under the tablecloth?
It was Friday night. We had returned from synagogue and
the candles were lit on the table. I escaped between the
slick mahogany legs and our chase resumed through the
bedrooms. Our father cuffed you on the ear for running
and I laughed. I was seven or eight then. You were closest
to me in years. We must have loved one another in those
dark rooms on Howard Street, Simon. People said we
looked like brothers. When I saw you in the hospital,
though, you could not have pounded my body with your
fists. You could not even bind your arms every morning
with your beloved black straps. Still, one year was enough,
Simon. I am sorry.

I smile and open my eyes. The door moves. Perhaps, I
think, perhaps I am wrong. Perhaps it pleased him to
have me tell the truth. He left me as he knew me. Would
I have been Harry Meyers if I had said yes? Simon, Simon.
You wanted to be pinched, didn't you, to make sure you
had not yet left this world. Well. Your brother did not
let you down. Miss Teitlebaum's head is in the doorway.

"What — ?" I ask.

Miss Teitlebaum smiles and apologizes for disturbing
me, but the substitute teacher in social studies is having
trouble with my official class. Mr. Vance, the Assistant
Principal, asked if I would look in. Her breasts move into
the room. She closes the door behind her. I cough and
bring up phlegm.

"If you'd like me to try — "

I swallow. "I'll go, I'll go."

Mr. Greenfeld's eyes open. Miss Teitlebaum smiles at him. Her chest rises. I lift my glasses and rub my eyes, at the corners.

"Do you want me to come along?"

"No, no. I will handle them. What room?"

"Four-twenty-five. The substitute is Miss Dabney — it's only her second time here. She's — "

I stand and take my briefcase. I push by Miss Teitlebaum, out the door. I walk to the right, then up one flight of stairs. I am pleased, I realize, to be needed in such a situation. I have been too gentle with my monkeys lately, I must admit. In the corridor I can hear the shouting. On the walls are pictures of Betsy Ross sewing a flag, of Washington crossing a river, of Lincoln dead in his memorial. A young woman stands outside a door. She is almost in tears. She tries to speak but I gesture to her to be silent. I do not want them to know I am approaching. I stop beside the room, then peer in through the window of the door. Ruben is standing on the teacher's desk, his arms outstretched, his short legs stamping out a wild dance as the monkeys clap for him. *"¡Mira! ¡Mira!"* they scream.

I push the door open. *"¡Cuidado!"* comes a shout from the back of the room. "Meyers!" I slam the door shut. Ruben laughs and does something with his hands. The students are quiet. Ruben is in another world, dancing furiously. He wears tennis sneakers. I set down my briefcase in the aisle and move toward him. *"¡Cuidado!* Ruben. *¡Mira!* . . . Meyers! Meyers!"* come the shouts. They do not disturb my wild-eyed one. I time my attack and snatch him by his left ankle. He lurches backwards and, as he throws something over my head to the others, he laughs. I pull at his leg and he loses his balance. "Be careful — " I call as he falls from the desk. I let go. He seems to stop in midair, to twirl like a ballet dancer. He lands lightly on the toes of his sneakers. He laughs again. His eyes are blazing now and he dances away from me, his feet moving with incredible speed. I see other eyes at the door, peering in. It is Manuel. Some students clap for Ruben, but I glare and they stop. He tries to sneak by me, but I push him back, then grab him by the wrist. Nobody speaks. Ruben's feet stop moving.

"Why were you absent from official class this morning?" I ask, tightening my grip on his wrist.

"I was there," he says. "You ask anybody."

"He was there — he was there — !" the students shout.

I grab his hair on the smooth side of his forehead and tug at it. "Nobody plays me for the fool, Ruben Fontanez," I say.

"I was there," he says again.

I see something move across the back row, from lap to lap. "Juan — bring that to me!" I drag Ruben down the aisle with me. He plants his feet and resists. I let go of his hair. "¡Ahora!" he shrieks, and then he yanks his wrist from my grip, dances lightly over my briefcase, and dashes from the room.

I will not catch him, I know. I take two strides and seize Juan by the back of the neck. Now that Ruben is gone, the students are quiet again. I do not have to apply much pressure. Juan reaches into his desk and brings forth a tiny doll. The other monkeys giggle. "What is this?" I demand. They are quiet. I let Juan go and I walk to the front of the room. The substitute teacher starts through the door but I motion to her to stay away. I look at my monkeys. They keep their eyes down, their heads bent. I look at the doll again, on the desk in front of me. It is about seven inches long, constructed of rags and adhesive tape and pipe cleaners. The head is made of papier mâché and it has been painted. Two long hatpins are stuck in the chest.

I pick up the doll and my eyes open wider. The evidence is unmistakable. The monkeys watch my expression, I know, but I cannot conceal my rage. The eyeglasses made from a paper clip, the large crooked nose, the graying hair. "Talk!" I say, and look out at my monkeys. "Talk or I will know what to do." They look down. "All right," I say, and walk up and down the aisles. I stop next to Rafael Quinones. He looks up at me briefly, almost smiles, then fixes his eyes on his desk. He is afraid. I grab the back of his flannel shirt and pull him out of his seat. "Hey — let go, man!" he cries. I twist his ear, then fix my grip along the sides of his neck. He squirms. "What you want with me? I no make the *muñecos* — " I squeeze harder. "Ruben — he make them of everyone. Last week he make one of me. He even make one of his mother — " He tries to sit, but knows it is no use. The others will not condemn him. It is no disgrace to give Harry Meyers information. "Every day he come in with a new one and go sticking pins in them." I squeeze. "This the first time he do one of you. That the truth — "

The monkeys jabber. "Go on," I say to Rafael. "More." He shrugs, and shakes his shoulders. His neck, I see, is filthy. His mustache is almost full grown. He stays in school until he is old enough to get working papers. "Let me go, man," he says. "I no make those voodoo dolls — " Behind me I hear laughter. I release Rafael and walk quickly to the door, but when I look out the corridor is deserted.

I stare at the doll. The room is silent. When the buzzer sounds, I let my monkeys proceed to their next class. I notice that the mouth Ruben has drawn seems to be smiling, curved around the bulbous head. I drop the doll into my briefcase.

The day moves on. Outside the sun is brighter. I assign written work to my classes and sit at my desk. I stare at the doll period after period, and find, despite myself, that I am developing an affection for my likeness. When the last period of the day is over and my official class returns to get their coats, Ruben is not with them. The bell rings and I escort my class to the exit. Across the street I see the old men. They are happy now. I return to my room and look at the doll again. It smiles at me. I remove the hatpins and let them drop to the bottom of my briefcase. I bend the two pipe cleaner arms forward, so that they are clasped, resting on the stomach, and I place the doll gently in the briefcase, beside my books.

In the main office I punch the time clock. I speak to no one but I am smiling broadly, more broadly than the likeness I carry with me. Students still linger near the school, smoking, talking, not wanting to return to their homes, to go to their jobs. I do not blame them. In a hallway I see a ninth grade Negro and a female monkey going at one another hungrily. That is all right also. I cross the street, toward the Brooklyn-Queens Expressway. Below the underpass there is fresh writing on the walls, in chalk, but I do not read the messages. The snow melts quickly. I feel strong. Harry Meyers is prepared to meet his cowboys.

THREE

In the distance, beyond the Expressway, I see the sun reflect from the dome of the Williamsburg Savings Bank. My body no longer aches. I unbutton my coat and walk past Broadway, under the pillars of the elevated subway. Perhaps, I think, I will even be able to sleep on my back tonight. The doors of stores are open now and the streets are busy with women shopping. From the open window of a Puerto Rican luncheonette come the odors of frying foods: bananas, pigs' tails, fish. I see one of my students, Jésus Martinez, of class 8-12, peddling his aluminum delivery cart in and out of the el pillars. His girl friend sits on top of the cart, chewing gum and reading a love-comic. Jésus sings.

I smile at them, but they do not see me. In the window of the *Botánica Religiosa* are statues of Jesus, gold crucifixes, religious candles. Beyond, where the sun dusts the inside of the store, herbs and hair applications and oils are arranged like medicines. A large black and orange sign advertises *Rocio Dama de Suerte*. An old woman smiles at me from behind a curtain, her face toothless. I cannot tell if she is Spanish or gypsy.

At the Yeshiva, I stop across the street and watch the cowboys playing in their schoolyard. The younger students are at work, pushing brooms across the concrete, cleaning the yard of puddles. It is like spring and once again I feel excited. My cowboys, with their black hats, their sidelocks, their fringed *tsitsis* flailing from their open shirts, are playing punchball and stickball and basketball as if they were ordinary American boys. They scream at the younger ones to keep the infield dry. A running cowboy is out as he arrives at second base. His hat falls to the ground. He picks it up, kisses it, tucks his sidelocks behind his ears and goes back to the sidelines, cursing. On the basketball court two cowboys are choosing with their fingers. Maybe, I think, maybe I will speak to Ruben and he will make Chassidic voodoo dolls. The thought pleases me. Mendel Kupietzky, reputed to be the great grandson of the legendary Reb Mendel, lofts a fly ball toward center field. It travels beyond the reach of Nachman Solovaychik, and lands in a puddle of slush and water. I laugh to myself. Mendel streaks around the bases, his hair uncurling from behind his ears. "Mad-Man Meyers!" I hear, and I know they have seen me.

It does not bother me, though. I swing my briefcase at my side and cross the street. Menachem Schiffenbauer sits on a folding chair behind home plate, waiting his turn, his head bobbing up and down as he reads from a huge leather-covered book. "Mad-Man Meyers! Mad-Man Meyers!" The cowboys are chanting in unison. Above the entrance to the Yeshiva, in blackening concrete, it is carved: "There Is Nothing in the World Which Does Not Contain a Commandment." My cowboys have taken up a new chorus. "Meyers is a *momzer* . . . Meyers is a *momzer*. . . ."

I laugh at them, caged inside their wire screen, and I enter the building. I smell raisin wine. The aroma is powerful and it cuts through the heavy air. The corridor walls are chipped and stained, the tile floor slippery. I hear the sound of men, complaining in Yiddish about mortgages, leases, tenants, interest rates. They are huddled in a tiny room and I pass them quickly. In a room next to them, young boys with the faces of old men sway back and forth amid piles of books as they chant their arguments to one another. At the end of the corridor a Negro janitor leans against a mop, a paper skullcap perched on the side of his head. I pass him and smell bourbon. "How ya doin', Rabbi?" he says to me. His eyes are glassy.

I descend to the basement. I open my locker and a cat leaps forward. It lands on a seat in the front row. Its back arches. I move toward it and it scampers from the room. On my desk is a sack of rotten apples. I remove it and I realize that I am still smiling. My cowboys enter the room, Menachem Schiffenbauer leading them. They sweat from their games, their eyes dance with mischief, but Harry Meyers is unaffected. This afternoon, I know, they cannot touch me.

They begin as usual: they shout, they throw things, they refuse to work, but it is nothing to me. I smile at them and they sense that something has changed. Even Menachem Schiffenbauer ceases to translate the mysteries of the Cabala. He looks at me from his deep blue eyes, perplexed. "I know something also," I say to him, and smile. My briefcase is beside my desk, my Spanish books are in front of me. I recite the lesson, lecturing to them on the irregular verb, *pedir. Pido, pides, pide* . . . My cowboys try to ignore me, but that is all right also. I continue. *Pida, pidas, pida, pidamos* . . . Old men pass our room, but they do not glance at us. They carry briefcases.

It is difficult to intimidate Harry Meyers, you see. The longer I go on, the quieter my cowboys become. I look at them, their shirts and vests covered with drippings of food. Their eyes begin to flicker. "Cowboys," I say. "Cowboys of the schoolyard. Mickey Mantle, Willie Mays — they would laugh at you also."

A piece of chalk flies by me, splintering against the blackboard. From the start it has amazed me, the passion they devote to their teams and heroes. I will tell you something: when it comes to memorizing statistics and records, they are geniuses. In the back row, Mordecai Fruchthandler rises and throws his Spanish book into the air. "*¡Bésame culo!*" he cries. The others giggle. I am unaffected. They stamp on the floor and pound on their desks. "*¡Bésame culo! ¡Bésame culo!*" they cry. "Cowboys," I whisper. "Cowboys of the schoolyard." They are listening to me, I know. "Sandy Koufax would laugh at you also."

The madness leaves their eyes. They turn to one another, helpless. Menachem Schiffenbauer does not look up. My cowboys are monkeys. I continue with the lesson and they repeat the words with me. "*Llegue, llegues, llegue, lleguemos* . . ." I assign a written exercise and they work quietly. I do not smile anymore. Well. They are boys, also, I suppose. I look down at them, at their heads covered with silk skullcaps, at the locks of hair which curl about their ears. They seem very small to me. When five-thirty comes they wait for me to dismiss them. Then they slink from the room, their Spanish books under their arms. Morris would be proud of me, I suppose, but such a thought does not give me much pleasure.

I am tired. I rest in my chair, the empty desks before me. I arrange their papers in a neat stack and put a paper clip on them. Outside it must already be dark. I open my briefcase, and put their papers inside. I take the doll in my hands and lift it from the briefcase. The pins rise from its chest in a "V." I tremble. The light seems to dim. The doll falls from my hands. It makes no noise. I look again, but I do not touch it. It rests on its back, smiling at me. I seize my briefcase and remove its contents, piling Hebrew books on Spanish books, papers on papers, but there are no hatpins at the bottom.

I replace my books, one by one, my eyes fixed on the doll. Its hands are clasped. The pins glisten. My heart pounds heavily. I put my overcoat on and then sit down to struggle with my galoshes. The doll watches me. I remember the note which came this morning and I feel Ruben's eyes, laughing at me. I place the doll carefully in my briefcase. I pull the zipper closed. I leave the room and start up the staircase. I wonder about the change that has come over my cowboys today. It was too easy, after all. Perhaps they were only pretending. Outside, they are waiting for me. I stop and go back down to the basement. The lights have been turned out and I feel my way along the corridor with my fingertips.

I turn the corner and in the Rebbe's room there is a

light. I look in. The Rebbe sits in a large maroon chair, his fur-trimmed hat tilted back as he sips wine and sings to himself. His eyes are closed, his beard is caked with dried food. His eyes open and he looks my way, but in the darkness he does not seem to see me. He holds his own face between his palms and he sings of the bird whose song of praise burst its own body. I do not move. He stands up and his eyes glow. Only the love of God will heal the hearts of mankind. He turns slowly in a circle and claps his hands, dancing lightly on his aged feet. He hops silently on one foot, in a circle. Around and around. He prays for all those who died to smuggle him from Poland during the Nazi occupation, of the Rebbes who masqueraded in his place so that he could make his way from country to country. He sings a song about each man who died while pretending to be him: in Budapest, in Rumania, in Greece, in Syria, in Palestine. He throws his head back and drinks, wine running down both sides of his mouth, into his beard. He slumps back into his chair, smiling. His eyes look through me. They close. He begins to snore.

I hurry past his room and out the side exit. My briefcase is heavy. The cowboys are not in sight. I breathe deeply. It has grown cold again and I button my coat to the top. I smell wine. I think back and wonder if there had been any time when one of the cowboys could have had access to my briefcase. I walk away from the Yeshiva, toward Marcy Avenue and the subway, trying to tell myself that nothing has happened, to clear my head, to shrug off what I have seen. But I cannot. I do not fool myself. At each corner, each tree, I expect to be attacked. I am shivering. The streets are empty.

I see Jackson's puzzled black face and I think of little

Gil, in the snow. The sight is a peaceful one. My heart slows. A woman yells in Spanish from a window overhead. *"¡Espéreme, batardo! ¡Ahora! ¡Espéreme!"* I try to recall the events of the day, one by one. Nobody, I am certain, could have touched my briefcase. I am on Broadway now and under the el pillars there is life. At the corners, groups of monkeys plan their evenings. Above me, a train roars through the night. The cold air has made my nose drip. I stop and look up, expecting to see the entrance to the subway, but I am at the wrong corner. Harry, Harry, it happens sooner than you think. I turn and walk back along Broadway. When I stop this time I am at Have-meyer Street. It is no use. If Jackson's brother is near, let him have me. I will not fight. I would never learn to sleep on my back anyway. My briefcase grows heavier and I switch hands. Danny, I suppose, will mourn for me.

There are no lights on in the store windows. The street corners are deserted. I hear no trains. The sidewalks are slippery from the ice. I hear giggling. Around the el pillars, cats move. When I am gone, I wonder if they will leave my story on the bulletin board. It is all right, Simon. It is all right. I am cold. I hear giggling again and glance to the right, squinting through my glasses. In the doorway of the Aponte Travel Agency two forms are locked to-gether. A neon sign flickers on and off, in red. I move closer. The giggling is that of a girl. A boy presses her against the window, his hands, I see now, working furi-ously under her sweater. The girl stares at me, over the boy's shoulder, and she chews gum. I cannot take my eyes from her. The boy is shorter than she is, coming to her chin only, and she seems, despite the paint on her face, to be no more than thirteen years old. There is a mole on her left cheek, and hairs grow from it. Still, she is lovely. I know her face, I realize. I step forward. In the doorway it is warmer. A poster advertises cut-rate family trips back to Puerto Rico. The girl chews and giggles. She has seen me. The boy's hands stop moving. He turns around.

It is my monkey. "Ruben!" I exclaim and rush forward. The girl slips away. Light dances from my monkey's eyes. He tries to escape but the doorway is too narrow. I corner him and press him against the window, my right hand at his throat.

"What you want?"

"You will come with me — " I say. He struggles. "You will come with me," I repeat. He kicks, but his foot hits the briefcase. "There are laws, Ruben," I say. "I have seen you also."

He squirms and his eyes do not look into mine. "I got to be home for supper," he says.

"I will buy you your supper." The words are out before I know it. Ruben's body goes limp. He eyes me, his head to one side. He smiles slowly.

"You mean it?" he asks.

"Yes," I say. I have no choice, after all. I know it at once. He touches my hand and I relax my grip. He does not try to run away. I think of the doll and I look closely at Ruben's face. His eyes look back at me now, and, in truth, they seem calm and innocent. "Yes," I say again.

We walk along Broadway and he stays a step behind me. Over a faded red flannel shirt, he wears only a thin denim jacket. He talks freely. He tells me about his younger brothers and sisters, his grandmother, his mother who is sick with a coughing sickness, the welfare man who is always checking on them. He says nothing about school. I feel pressure on the sides of my head, at the temples.

The first restaurant we come to is a Chinese one and we enter and take a booth at the back. He blows into his cupped hands to warm them. I hang up my overcoat, but I leave my briefcase under the table, next to my feet. Ruben tells me about the way his mother beats him when he is bad.

"But she getting pretty weak now," he says. My eyes tear from the cold. "She make these funny noises from her chest. She real sick, Mister Meyers. It worse now, with the winter." He seems very much at ease. His face is open. "She keep trying to get us in a project where you get more heat, but you got to have a husband to get into the project. That's the rules of the welfare." The waiter comes and I order for us. Ruben is laughing now, pleased with himself. "I make one of the dolls of the man from the welfare!" He shakes his head. "It don't help. They say to call when things go bad but you live on the welfare, you not allowed to have a phone."

I nod.

"She a real sick woman," Ruben says, and briefly, I see his eyes flash. "Real sick." I remember what Rafael said about the doll of his mother. Our soup comes and Ruben begins drinking it, carefully at first, then with increasing abandon. He looks up at me and smiles. "It's warm," he says. I watch him as I sip mine and I feel myself relax. I too am warm inside. "This soup real crazy," he says. I smile and I say to myself: after all, Harry, he is only a boy.

"Is this your first time in such a restaurant?" I ask. He nods, his mouth full. "Is it all right for you to be here?" I say. "Perhaps your mother will worry that you are not at home."

"She don't care," he says. "I only make trouble for her, she says. It easier when we not all around."

When the main dish comes, he hardly looks at me and that is all right also. I watch him devour his food and I eat from my own plate, pausing now and then to sip tea. I am feeling somewhat better. My nose has stopped running and my eyes are dry. I feel very tired, though. It has been a long day. It would not be so terrible if Harry Meyers could trade in some of his parts, I think. My toes are numb. I remember the dinner with Danny. My muscles tighten. I look down and think of the wrinkles Ruben has drawn on the bulbous head. While he eats I open the briefcase. He talks about his friend Manuel Alvarez who came on the boat with him from Puerto Rico. I am not interested. I take the doll from the briefcase and I keep it under the table, on my lap. My chest hurts and I realize I have been eating too fast. I drink some cold water.

"I seen you," Ruben says. "Me and Manuel."

I do not respond to his statement. It is time, you see. My right hand moves. I thrust the doll in front of my monkey's face. "Did you do this — ?" I ask.

He nods. "You know I did. I real sorry, Mister Meyers," he says. "I no mean nothing. That the truth. You a pretty good teacher."

He goes back to his food. I slap his fork away and it clinks to the floor. "What about the pins?" I ask. It is difficult to whisper, to keep my voice low. "The pins, Ruben — "

He bends away from me and picks his fork up from the floor. He wipes it on a napkin. I look around the corner of our booth. The restaurant is almost empty. At a corner table a Chinese family eats quietly, a large brown fish on a platter in the middle of their table. The waiters sit near them, eating their own supper, their rice bowls raised to their mouths. "The pins, Ruben. The pins — "

He shrugs. "I no mean nothing," he repeats. "I telling you the truth. That just to have some fun. I do it of everybody — "

I lay the doll down and reach across the table, grabbing my monkey's wrist. My heart pounds unevenly. "Before," I say. "I took the pins out. Who put them back in — ?"

He shrugs again. "I told you I no mean nothing," he says, and twists his wrist loose. "That the truth." His eyelids drop. "After you catch me in the room I get out of that school real quick and go down to the river to see the boats break up the ice."

He looks at me and his eyes are soft and puzzled. They are a true monkey's eyes. The doll is between us, next to the pot of tea. There is nothing else to say, I realize. I breathe in. The doll seems very small. I place it next to me, on the plastic cushion. I drink some tea to calm myself. "This food real crazy," Ruben says again. "I got to come back here." I touch the doll and unclasp its hands. Harry, Harry, you are playing the fool. Enough. I put the doll back in the briefcase. Ruben smiles at me. I wonder about Danny's questions concerning next year. "You talk to him sometime and you see." Ruben is speaking.

"I will see what?" I ask.

"That Manuel not so C.R.M.D. like people think." Brown sauce drips down my monkey's chin. "I tell you something — he know the lifetime batting averages of every Spanish ballplayer." I relax somewhat. "We see you lots, me and Manuel, where we work."

"You see me?" I gather my last bit of fried rice together with a fork.

"Where you live — " His eyes dance. "It surprise you,

c

what we do to make money." He puts his chin close to his plate and sweeps the last bit of food into his mouth. "You can get a lot of things if you got money."

We are quiet. In the half-yellow light of the restaurant his forehead does not seem ugly. I taste garlic and think of Nydia and Carlos. I picture her eyes, downcast, as she passes along the staircase. Ruben asks me why I am in Williamsburg at such a late hour. I picture Nydia when I saw her the first time, the day she returned from the hospital, smiling shyly, asking if I wanted to look at the baby. I tell Ruben that I am a teacher of cowboys. At the word cowboys he laughs. The baby was wrapped in a soft blue blanket. Carlos' grandmother was there also. I explain to my monkey that I teach them Spanish and he laughs even more. I lean forward and tell him that I do it for the money. Harry Meyers will never be obligated to anybody's welfare. Ruben sets his jaw and nods. On Friday nights, he says, he and Manuel and Manuel's sister listen outside the windows of the Yeshiva. He speaks with passion of the way the cowboys dance and sing, and of how Manuel tries to imitate them. He cannot wait to tell Manuel what I have named them.

Our dessert comes. I wonder also: what will I do next year. Ruben uses the word cowboy and I laugh with him. I tell him about Morris's fears. Ruben does not laugh. "They got magic, Mister Meyers," he says. "I seen them." I remember the story Morris and I laughed at when we were boys: about the Rebbe who was such a cowboy that, although he had ten children, he did not know his wife had a wooden stump for a leg until her funeral. Ruben's eyes are bright. The cowboys are harmless, I assure him. I think of Rabbi Akiba, who set out from home when he was already forty years old, to learn to read and write. Later his wife was plagued by his disciples, who demanded details of his behavior during intercourse. Ruben is talking about Manuel's sister. Her name is Mara Alvarez and she is in a special school for Catholic girls.

"Ah, Ruben, Ruben," I say, looking at him across from me. "Tell me something, Ruben Fontanez. What will you be doing in ten years?"

"I be making it — "

"No, Ruben," I say. "Listen to me. What will you be *doing?*" He shrugs and eats from his plate of ice cream. I know what it is I have been waiting for, you see, what I want to say to him. "Ruben, listen to me," I say again. "Put down your spoon and listen." He does as I ask, and his eyes tell me that it is true, that I can reach him, that he will hear me. I think of Rabbi Akiba and though I know such a thought is silly, I proceed. I lean toward him and whisper. "Listen, Ruben Fontanez. You must get an education. Do you understand? You must get out of Williamsburg. Harry Meyers is telling you something. Do you hear me?" His eyes do not blink. He wipes his lip with a finger. "Listen to me, Ruben Fontanez. If you do not get an education and get out, do you know what you will be? In ten years, in twenty years, in thirty years — ? It will be the same forever, Ruben. Until your body dries up. You will be a filthy monkey with filthy children all around you. You will all be hungry. Do you hear me?" The door of the restaurant opens. The Chinese family is leaving. The cold air from the outside reaches us and I shiver. "In ten years, Ruben, your life will be at an end. You will be drunk half the time. Your children will cry in your ears. Your friends will be in jail. You will be loving somebody else's wife and yours will be grabbing the plumber. You will be making fifty dollars a week and your nights will be endless." I am not sure I have meant to say all these things, but it is all right. Sarah is pleased. I feel pressure on my eyes. My feet are cold. "Do you hear me?" His face is serious. He nods and blinks his eyes, then nods again, slowly. "You are still a boy — enjoy life, have fun," I continue. "But get out, Ruben!" The words come with a rush of air. "Do you hear me?" I breathe out, exhausted.

"I listening to you," he says. "I listening, Mister Meyers." Then he smiles at me, and, my heart full, I reach across the table and take his hand, pressing it.

He finishes his ice cream and we do not talk again until we are outside. I walk alongside him and he asks if I would like to see where he lives. I nod, and we walk on, under the el pillars, my briefcase at my side. It is cold, but I do not mind. Ruben is talking about Manuel's sister again and he wants to know if I have ever seen her. I say that I have not. He tells me that she is very beautiful. We turn a corner and walk down a dark street. "That girl you catch me with," Ruben says, embarrassed, "that not Manuel's sister. I want you to know." He would like to tell me more, but I do not encourage him. It is his business.

"It pretty bad in the winter, when you got no place warm to go to. Sometimes you sneak into the movies, but that not so good." I smell garlic again, and the odors of frying fish. Ahead of us, I see lights. I hear the sounds of electric guitars and tambourines. In the front doors of buildings, people chatter in Spanish. A bottle crashes to the sidewalk behind us. A baritone voice rises above the sound of electric guitars, of portable radios.

"No me olvides . . . porque lo quiero . . . no me olvides. . . ."

"This my block," Ruben says. He seems sad now. I remark on the music, the spirit of his neighborhood, but my remarks, I know, are feeble. He shrugs. "It not so nice to be poor," he says. "What you said before." He points to the third story of an old tenement. There are flowerpots on the fire escape, a candle in the window. I see the shape of a heavy woman, silhouetted, rocking a child in her arms. "That's where I live," he says.

"Ah, Ruben, Ruben," I say. "I must go."

"Thank you for the food, Mister Meyers," he says.

"Thank you, Ruben — " I begin, and, impulsively, I lean down, and not without tenderness, kiss him on the forehead.

He smiles up at me in the dim light, and suddenly his eyes are on fire again. He laughs and leaps away from me. *"¡Maricón!"* he shouts. *"¡Viejo!"* He dances around me, screaming. Windows above us open. His eyes are the eyes that were in the classroom when he held the doll. People call from the windows. I hear music. "Ruben—?" I ask. "Why — ?" He laughs again. *"¡Anciano!"* a woman shouts down at me. "Go home. For shame. Go home!" "Ruben?" I plead. He dances around me, making mysterious motions. He runs at me, then retreats. *"¡Pato! ¡Pato!"* I hear. *"¡Maricón! ¡Maricón!"* Ruben charges at me and snatches my briefcase. "He kiss me and hold my hand!" he shouts to the open windows. They hurl down abuse. I look up at the faces of monkeys, on both sides of the street now, leaning over fire escape railings. Ruben comes at me again, holding the doll in his hand, outstretched. "Give it to me," I say. "Please — " He jumps up and down, his feet moving with miraculous speed. I hear drums beating. From the entrance to Ruben's building, a crowd moves toward me. One man has a belt wrapped around his fist. His shirt is open, revealing a massive chest. I shudder. I see the doll. The drums are louder. Then Ruben is standing next to me. He puts the doll back into the briefcase and hands it to me. "Run!" he whispers. "I see you soon. Where you live." I look at him. "Run!" I try to touch him, to question him. "Run!" he says. "Run!"

I turn and do as he says. The shouts follow me down the street, Ruben's voice above them all, laughing. "¡Maricón! . . . Maricón . . ." I race down dark streets, the screams behind me, and I do not stop until I am on the platform of the elevated subway. I stand in the shadows. My heart pounds heavily and I fear for my life. On each side of my chest there is a sharp pain. I see the lights of the train, as it curls toward me from the open sky. I board it. Nobody follows me. The train goes over the Williamsburg Bridge and I do not look out the windows. At Delancey Street I change for the uptown IND. In the next car I see a boy who looks like Manuel, leaning forward and puffing on a cigarette. A policeman comes through, but I do not look at his face.

At 72nd Street I get out. I pass Verdi Square and the Dori Donut Shop without raising my eyes. On my own street, outside the Park West Hospital, there is another policeman. Someday, I think, someday the police will guard all the hospitals, they will be assigned to the waiting rooms of doctors, the corridors of laboratories. It is coming. Believe me. In my building I hear Carlos and Nydia screaming at one another. I hurry by their apartment, and up the stairs. A telephone is ringing. I unlock my door but I do not answer the phone. I put my briefcase down on my desk and undress quickly. Tomorrow. What will I do tomorrow, I wonder. I lie on my back in the darkness and I think about next year. Tomorrow I will telephone Mrs. Davies and tell her to get a substitute teacher. I get up and drink some water, but it does not help. The pains in my chest are worse. Warm milk would be good. There is no milk in the refrigerator, though. Perhaps Morris is right. Perhaps it would be best. I feel Ruben's eyes upon me. I see the doll, smiling. My phone rings again. I count. It rings eleven times, then stops. When the Muslims governed Spain they were good to the Jews. That is no small thing. I should let my cowboys know. I remember the party my father made every year to celebrate the Emperor Franz Joseph's birthday. All the neighbors and relatives came. I drank wine until I fell asleep. I will telephone Mrs. Davies. It is settled. I will stay at home and read, in Spanish. It has been a long time since I read *Don Quixote de la Mancha.* The pains spread through me. It is no use. I pull the covers around me and turn onto my side, then to my stomach. My nose drips onto my pillow. The telephone begins ringing again. I draw the pillow closer to me. My toes are cold. Ruben, Ruben. Listen to me, Ruben Fontanez.

FOUR

I HAVE BEEN SLEEPING on my side, but I do not look behind. I can feel Sarah there, with me, her body pressing
on the bed. My head is heavy, my sinuses are still clogged.
I pull the blanket closer to my neck. The parts of the
dream that I can remember are vivid. The cowboys were
in it and they danced around me endlessly, chanting Chassidic melodies, their arms on one another's shoulders, hopping lightly, smiling. Their beards grew from the tops of
their heads. Their chins were bare. I turned with them.
You were with me, Sarah. Then we were outside the circle,
watching them from the window of our apartment on
Eastern Parkway as they danced over the lawns of the
Botanic Gardens and made their way up the walls of the
Brooklyn Museum. You told me not to worry, you stroked
my cheeks, you whispered softly in my ears. You spoke to
me in Spanish. It was my birthday present, you said. You
had been studying at the library. You wanted to share my

work with me. You promised you would never speak English again. The lights were coming on in the museum and the cowboys were dancing up the walls. Stay with me, Sarah. I am cold. You want me to speak in Spanish, but I will not. I am an American, Sarah, the accident of my father's old age. Do you hear me? You lead me to the bed and it is warm there. I smell bacon frying. You hold me close and the flesh between your thighs is loose and warm. *No me olvides, querido* Harry, you say. *Muy amado mio.* Do not forget me. Sarah, Sarah. I think I hear the cowboys on the sides of our building, pecking at the windows, scaling the fire escapes with ropes. You tell me not to worry and I huddle close under the covers, warming my ears at your breasts.

I do not look behind. The room is ice-cold. I am, at least, sleeping on my side. It is something. Light enters from under the window shades. I hear a car pass below. I know it is foolish, but I am afraid to turn over, afraid I will find you there, smiling at me, brushing your gray hair. You handed the pigeon to me and I remember holding its softness as it gurgled beneath my fingertips. Your thighs are as soft. I wonder if the pigeon was in the dream. Here on West 76th Street I have no fire escape. The cowboys are singing with great strength and the auditorium at the Brooklyn Museum is crowded with members of my family. Light shines on them from the dome overhead. I cannot see Simon. They are singing the song my father hummed on the couch. I move further under the covers and Sarah wraps her legs around mine. I am an old man, Sarah. Do you hear me? I ache for you. I admit it. Above your knees, I warm my hands. The cowboys are singing in the branches of the trees that line Eastern Parkway,

c*

stroking their naked chins. Sarah tells me I should shave, and she laughs softly. I keep my hands warm. I turn over and face her, her features distinct under the covers, and I move to the point where her thighs begin. The flesh is warm. I hear giggling, then more laughter. The light goes on under the covers and where my love would enter, I see the face of Ruben's doll, staring out between the hair of a cowboy's beard, laughing hideously.

Pains move through my chest. My mouth goes slack. Sarah's arms comfort me and I am a child again. It is only a doll, she tells me. I will not open my eyes again. I swear it, Sarah. I turn away and she presses against me from behind. Her body is still warm. The doll laughs. Outside, the cowboys swing in their branches. Across the street, the concert goes on. The room is black. Sarah, Sarah. It happens so soon. I am sorry. Believe me. I hear the cowboys singing my father's song. Their voices grow louder.

I reach my right hand from under the covers and scratch on the floor beside my bed. I find my shoe and lift my watch from inside. It is almost seven. I will have to call Mrs. Davies again this morning. Today I will tell her. There will be no more calls from Harry Meyers. He has enough sick leave accumulated to last him until his retirement. He is entitled. When he wants to return he will call you. I lay the watch on my night table and pull the blanket tight around my neck. I cough and bring up phlegm, then I swallow. The radiator knocks. There are footsteps outside my door. I hear the sound of the toilet flushing. My own bladder is full. If I tell Morris that I was able to sleep on my side he will say it is because I am staying away from the cowboys. He will be here after breakfast, with a sweet roll brought from the kitchen of his home. I will not refuse it, I can assure you. And he will not press me about buying the bed next to his. He sees my situation now. He knows when words are not needed.

But I will fool him, you see. Harry Meyers will return to his monkeys and cowboys. It is merely a question of time. I will use up some of my sick leave, I will recover from my cold, I will regain my strength. I swallow and feel the glands move along my throat. If I have such dreams only to sleep on my side, I think, I have a good deal to look forward to when I reach my back. But that is all right also. Everything has its price in this world. There are rules and regulations.

The telephone rings again, but it does not bother me. I will settle that soon enough. If it rang after midnight last night Harry Meyers did not hear it. His sleep has been deep and heavy. I thank you for that, Sarah. From under the windows the radiator begins to send its heat across my room. I stay on my side now, the pillow beneath my shoulder, under my cheek. Perhaps I will shave this morning. I shift my weight and hear a mattress spring uncoil. My side of the bed goes down slightly. There is more light in the room, slipping through the window shades. I rub my eyes and laugh at myself, remembering the dream. Forget it, Harry, I say. But I do not fool myself. I was frightened. You are with me still, Sarah, and I do not forget the sensation, the feel of your warm flesh, the sight of the doll.

I close my eyes and think of the hours that lie in wait for me, until it is time to sleep again. In truth, I do not know what I will do with them. I have already read *Don Quixote* twice within the last ten days. I read it in Spanish, something I have not done since before the war, when I assigned it to the bright students in my honor classes. I will tell you something: here is a book. It is no accident that Cervantes died on the same day as Shakespeare, Harry Meyers would tell his classes. But you too were a fool, Miguel de Cervantes Saavedra, to have placed all your hopes on a post in the American colonies. What Morris says is true: a curse on Columbus that he ever discovered this land. It was not so terrible that you rested in the jails of Seville, that your government did not let you come here to redeem your failures. Still, I have had enough of your book. I will save it to give to my monkey. I will tell him that you called yourself the one-handed man — *"El Manco de Lepanto."* That will please him, I know. He will stick pins in your other hand.

I open my eyes and glance at the mantel of the fireplace, where the doll rests now, smiling at me. In truth, I have grown fond of my likeness. I would not be without it. You are right, Sarah. It is only a doll. And a dream is only a dream.

I ease my feet out from under the covers and slide them along the floor until they find their slippers. They are the old Persian slippers, the birthday gift you gave me so many years ago. The radiator under the window groans, iron on iron. I let the covers fall from my back and I slip quickly into my bathrobe, pulling it tightly around me. I glance back at the bed, walk away, then look at it again. It is too narrow, of course. You sleep alone, Harry Meyers.

At the window, I raise the shade and warm my hands above the radiator. The window sash swings gently from side to side. Across from me, in the upper floors of the other brownstone buildings, shades are still down. It is all right, I think. They are entitled also. For block after block, you see, all along the west side of Manhattan island, the single rooms in the top floors of the brownstones and graystones are paid for from social security checks. Harry Meyers' situation is not so unusual. Perhaps he will get together with others and form a union. Next year, I think. When I retire.

Already, you see, they are trying to move us out. It is difficult to grow rich from other people's social security. Across the street, toward Amsterdam Avenue, numbers 171 and 173 have been boarded up. The wreckers have gutted the insides. The walls and floors are gone. Only the fronts and the roofs remain. I questioned the workmen one time, but they would give no information. I predict an apartment house, with no fourth or fifth floors for the members of our union. In truth, Morris's arguments gain strength each day.

Perhaps if we get more students to move onto the floors with us, we will be able to organize more effectively, to protest. On top of me, I know, is an Oriental, a graduate student at Columbia. But he never says hello to me. He carries brown grocery bags in and out of his room and lets wonderful odors trail through the stairwell. Well. If he does not wish to greet me, that is his business. Below me, I see the men walking to the synagogue, their prayer bags under their arms. It amazes me, to tell the truth, that they do not get bored, repeating their journeys every day, reciting the same prayers. I assure you, Simon, I would not have lasted more than two months, even if I had tried. Believe me.

I do not think about what I will do next year. What I will do for the next fourteen or fifteen hours seems more important. I have my two telephone calls to make. Morris will be here. Nydia will come upstairs with the baby and some food. I will watch the street below. I will cook meals over my gas burner. And I will consider: the first thirty years of my life as compared to the years sixty through ninety. When one makes such a comparison, it becomes clear that Harry Meyers may not, after all, be such a fool. One day past sixty-nine is all he asks for.

Ahead of me, at an equal distance from the window, I see my reflection, suspended over West 76th Street. Even Danny would not be able to say to me that I am looking good. These past ten days have not been easy. So. I will rest for the remainder of this week. There is Thursday and Friday. Then the weekend. Perhaps I will return to school on Monday. But we will see. It is not such a bad thing that I try my room for a while. This year can be next year.

Directly under the window Carlos exits and, as he crosses the street, he drums on the hood of a black car with his fingertips. He passes the old garbage-can woman and says good morning. She ignores him and I watch as she works her way up the street, from garbage can to garbage can, filling the shopping bags that sag from both her arms. One of the men on his way to the synagogue tries to give her some money, but she pushes him away. It does not surprise me. What good is a piece of green paper, after all, when you are searching for lost treasure.

I raise the shade of my other window and then move back into my room. I smooth down the sheets on my bed, and over the blankets I arrange the blue chenille bedspread. Sarah looks at me from the dresser, the two of us framed in silver, leaning toward one another, standing under the willow tree in the Botanic Gardens. Behind us is a brook and in the distance you can see the hothouses. My walls are without pictures. Perhaps when the year ends, I think, I will take the contents of the glass-enclosed bulletin board with me. You cannot fool yourself for long, Harry Meyers. You have been leaving your walls bare for a good reason. Soon. Soon they will receive their proper covering. Danny will be pleased. He and Jean can come to dinner then.

It is something to consider, I tell myself, as I run the water from the faucet into my teapot. The school may protest, but when Harry Meyers can no longer stand in front of a class, there will be nothing of him in a school building, I promise you that. If they have copies made, that is their business. I cannot stop them. The original, though, will stay with me.

On my gas burner the water boils and I drop tea leaves to the bottom of the pot, then turn the flame off. I leave the room and go to the bathroom in the hall. There is a slight burning sensation as I relieve myself. I credit this to my swollen glands. I wonder what my cowboys are doing without me, or if they have hired a teacher to take my place. There is a pattering of feet and as I exit a door closes at the rear of the landing. One day I will corner you also, Mrs. Wenger, and make you tell me your story. I will get Morris to put you on his list. At your age, you would be a fine investment for his home.

I open the door to my room, then close it without going inside. I wait. Mrs. Wenger steps from her room and when she sees me standing opposite her, no more than twenty feet away, her toothless mouth opens in surprise. I try to see into her room, behind her. Her bathrobe is made of black silk, and she pulls it tightly around her withered body. But she does not move forward or backward. I start to smile, but my lips quiver. In the lines of her face I sense only one thing: she will not move. We have been neighbors for eight years, Mrs. Wenger, ever since that dark night your young couple deposited you here with much whispering. I nod good morning. We should speak to one another, Mrs. Wenger. She does not move. I try to smile again. Her knuckles are white where she clutches her robe. All right. Enough. I turn and open the door to my own room. I hear her take a step. I look back and she stops. I shrug, my hands up, my palms exposed. "I am an old man," I say.

In my room I chew on a piece of rye bread and drink tea. The tea warms my chest. I go to the window and, in the bottom of the boarded-up buildings across the street I see what looks like a small fire. Shadows move swiftly across the rubble. I rub my eyes and look again. I see nothing. It is only the early morning sun playing tricks, I tell myself.

Below me the prayers are ended and the men return from the synagogue. At number 171, between the fourth and fifth floors, tucked in the corner, where the buildings join, I see that your face is still there, Sarah. Do not worry, my wife. The wreckers will not get you. Amid the baroque stone carvings, you gaze at me, your cheek sandblasted, soot in your hair. I had lived here for five years before I noticed you, among the shadows and stained glass. My eyes wander over the buildings to either side of you, up and down their faces, tracing the outlines of useless ornaments, of cupids and lions' heads and medallions. They will not get you. Believe me, Sarah.

I telephone Mrs. Davies and tell her that I am still sick.

She starts to tell me that all the teachers are concerned about my health, but I cut her off. I tell her that she will get no more telephone messages from Harry Meyers. I do not care about regulations. When I am ready to return I will be in touch. If there are emergencies, I have a mailbox.

It is past eight o'clock. I dial the business office of the telephone company and tell them what to do. I am pleased with my decision. It is a start, at least. I feel my throat, gently, and find that my glands, under my jawbone, are not as enlarged as they have been. The lumps wiggle under my fingers. My buzzer startles me. I ring back, but I am puzzled. It is too early for Morris, and Nydia does not need to ring from outside. I rub my unshaven cheek with my fingertips. If it is Jackson's brother, I realize, I am not ready for him yet. Even these ten days have not been enough. I would like more time. That is not so much to ask, after all.

I go to the door and double-lock it, then press my ear to the wood. Someone is taking the stairs two at a time. The footsteps are light and there is more than one person. I am certain of it. The steps reach my landing and stop. They approach my door and there is a rapping of knuckles on wood. I do not answer. I hear the shuffling of feet. They whisper. The knocking comes again, louder. "It's me — " I recognize the voice at once. I should not be surprised. "Open up quick, Mister Meyers. You got to. Please — "

I step away from the door and I tie the belt of my robe more tightly. The knocking comes again. "Please, Mister Meyers, you got to let me in quick. I telling you the truth — "

I will not touch the doorknob. I can see the cowboys

swinging in the trees, humming to each other. I look at the window, but there are no branches there, no leaves. Only the faces of other brownstones. I remember the way the pigeon felt in my palms. "Go away," I say. "Go away, Ruben Fontanez." But I am not certain, after, that I have spoken the words aloud. I move backwards into my room. I lift my teacup and drink, but the tea is already cool. I shiver. Morris is right. The knocking is more insistent. The doll on the fireplace smiles. It is all too ridiculous. The light from the window flashes from the pins as if they are made of silver. A dream is only a dream, Harry.

"You got to let me in, Mister Meyers." He pauses. "It's my mother." I do not move. "That the truth — "

I breathe in deeply. I can hear my heart. I am glad, at least, that my bed is made, my room neat. Go away. Go away, Ruben Fontanez. The cowboys stroke their beards. I wonder if I should have said what I did about Sandy Koufax. That was foolish, Harry. Someone is moving away from the door. "Okay," Ruben says. "I tell you why so you listen to me." I wait. *Mi madre,* Mister Meyers. *¡Mi madre es muerto!* That the truth. *Mi madre,* Mister Meyers. I telling you — "

His voice is desperate. The room seems to tilt slightly. I cannot stop myself, you see. I fumble at the lock and pull the door open. Ruben steps into the room and I lock the door behind him. He glides swiftly to the windows and looks down, then up.

"I lost him," Ruben says. He smiles at me and his eyes are soft. "You should of seen us go in and out of the subways," he says, shaking his head. "We too fast for them — "

I stay by the door. "I am sorry," I begin.

Ruben nods. "Like I tell you when we eat together: she real sick." For a second I think I see something glow in his eyes. "Real sick — " He walks around my room, observing, touching the furniture. He inspects the opening to the fireplace and taps on the black iron that has sealed it shut. He picks up the doll. "You still got this — "

I nod.

"I tell you the truth," he says. "Of all the ones I do, this my favorite." He fondles the head and rearranges the paper-clip eyeglasses. "It really look like you, you know? My art teacher, she say I got talent, I should be a real artist someday, for money — " He puts the doll down, crosses the room and lifts the picture from the dresser. "This your wife?" he asks, but before I can answer, the picture is back on the dresser and Ruben is at my sink, taking a glass of water for himself. "This place not so bad," he says. "It be better if they open up the fireplace."

He drinks the glass of water in one swallow and wipes his mouth with the back of his hand. "They got all the others," he says. "That why I got to come here." He sits down on the edge of my bed and looks at me. "I got no place to go to, Mister Meyers." He rests his head in his hands. I am wary. I would like to see the expression in his eyes. "That why I come here. I got nobody. I been hiding out in places for three days now, and I thinking a lot about what I done to you — you know?" He does not look up. "I figure I got to take a chance and come speak with you." The light from the window glances off his forehead. I sit down now, in my easy chair, across the room from him. In my ears there is a high-pitched ringing sound. "I remember what you say to me," he says.

"I am sorry about your mother," I offer.

He shrugs and glances toward the window. I follow his eyes to the rooftops across the street. "They want to put me in one of them places for guys who got no parents — "

"An orphanage," I say.

He nods. "I tell you the truth, Mister Meyers. I kill myself before I go to one of them places. I hear stories about what they do to you there." He shakes his head up and down, and moves from the bed. His eyes look straight at me. "I promise you one thing, Mister Meyers — someday I gone to go there and get my brothers and sisters out — "

I can feel his breath on me. "You — you cannot stay here," I say.

He moves away from me, to the window. For an instant, he seems puzzled. Then he laughs. "You think I come here for that?" He rubs his chin and continues to laugh to himself. He stops and eyes me. "I tell you before — I just come to talk with you about what I gone to do with my life. I remember what you say to me in the restaurant. I was listening, Mister Meyers. Like I tell you — "

There is something in his voice which makes me uneasy. I see his reflection in the window. "I remember what happened, also," I say, with more firmness. "Do not play games with me, Ruben Fontanez."

His eyes are on me. The light at the window is too bright for me to see his face. Behind me, at the door, I hear a scratching sound. "Okay," Ruben says. "I tell you the real truth, Mister Meyers." He is sitting on the bed again. "I hear you not been in the school and I think maybe it because of what I did — so I want to see for myself — " He is up from the bed again. He examines my desk. He picks up the copy of *Don Quixote* but it does not interest him and he leaves it. "Like I tell you, we see you here, where you live. We work around here sometimes, so I figure I stop by to make sure."

The sound at the door disturbs me, but my monkey does not seem to hear it. He tells me of the mistake he made three days ago, when they buried his mother. He should not have gone, he says. "They almost get me, but I too fast for them." He is laughing. He stands by the fireplace, touching my likeness with his fingertips. "I guess you not supposed to think it funny, in a place like that, but they chase me all over, through the flowers and things — "

The noise at the door is more insistent. Ruben glances toward it. He asks if it is all right, but he does not wait for an answer. When he opens the door, I stand and pull at the belt of my robe. Another monkey is there, crouched low. Ruben whispers to him. The monkey enters behind Ruben, slouching, and moves silently to a corner of the room, next to the window. He squats and draws in on a cigarette so that the hollows in his cheeks show.

Ruben asks me if I know Manuel Alvarez and I nod. His body seems to be made of sticks and his eyelids hang down. "Manuel is my good friend," Ruben says. "He work with us for the money." He puts a hand on Manuel's shoulder. "When they chasing me all around, he keep the stuff for me, even though it scare him." Then Ruben is next to me, his hand in front of my eyes. He whispers. "You know what I got? Aiee — they not be able to do nothing to me when I got this!"

The room is too warm and I feel sleepy again. The smoke from Manuel's cigarettes lingers near the ceiling. Morris will be here soon. He will know if this is happening or not. You can depend on Morris. I will have him deliver a message to Danny. Ruben's hand is in front of my lips now. He opens it, revealing a black palm. *"Mi madre,* Mister Meyers," he whispers. He curls his fingers over the dirt and his hand trembles. *"¡Mi madre!"* His hand opens again and the lumps of earth are under my nose. I sniff but I can smell nothing. "This from my mother's grave, Mister Meyers." He skips backwards and spins around. His feet move lightly. He shows the earth to Manuel and Manuel slides away. He grinds his cigarette out under his heel and lights another one, sucking on it. *"¡Bruja! ¡Bruja!"* Ruben breathes as he circles the room. He looks through the window at the street below and shakes his fist at it. *"¡Bruja!"* he sings. *"¡Bruja!"* He turns his head toward me, over his shoulder. "Those dolls just for fun," he says. "With this I gone to be able to work real *brujeria* — like Señora Rosa from our village."

He crouches down next to Manuel and speaks with great gentleness. "You remember Señora Rosa, Manuel. From the island — " Manuel seems to nod, but I cannot be sure. Ruben turns away from him and searches the surface of my desk. He finds an envelope and asks if it is all right to use it. I nod. He pours the earth into the envelope, then licks it closed and puts it carefully into his side pocket. "They be waiting for me, Mister Meyers. They see me take the dirt. That when the man from the place come after me. I run fast. Manuel, he waiting for me behind a grave and I give it to him in his pocket." He rubs his hand over Manuel's head, and whispers to him in Spanish, telling him how brave he was. He assures him that there is no danger. Only the person who steals the earth has the power to summon the dead person's spirit.

He has told him this before, I can tell, but Manuel is not yet convinced.

"You will see, Mister Meyers — when the right time comes, I gone to work great *brujería,* like Señora Rosa — "

Manuel's eyelids move upwards. "Only I got to wait for the right time. It only good one time — " I am thinking of Jackson again, and I can see his blue earmuffs. I would like to laugh. There should be pictures for the cowboys also, I think, to line their corridors. "You know what?" Ruben says. "I think the reason I come here really is just to show you — " He taps his side pocket. Manuel does not move. His eyes are on the roofs of the buildings across the street. "You think it just silly, I bet — "

"No," I begin.

"It's okay," Ruben says. He is silent suddenly. He sits on the bed, leaning forward. He speaks again and his voice has changed. "How you been feeling?" he asks. "I sorry I forget to ask — "

"It is only a cold," I say.

"If you need something, that the reason we here," he says. "To get you what you need." Manuel stops puffing on his cigarette. Across the street, he has seen something. I go to the telephone and lift the receiver. Ruben stands and moves toward me, then freezes. There is no mistaking the look in his eyes. Well. Mad-Man Meyers has a few weapons left. Manuel moves deeper into his corner, his chin at his chest. "I am just checking," I explain, and I hold the receiver toward Ruben. There is no sound. "Listen — it has been disconnected."

Ruben relaxes. "You got any kids?" he asks. Manuel's eyes return to the window.

"No," I say.

"That not so good." My monkey shakes his head. "When you get old you won't have nobody to take care of you. They put you away, like they did my grand-mother — " He taps on the desk with his knuckles. "When they get her, I know what coming — "

"No," I say. "I was married late, you see. I was past thirty. And my wife, she — "

"You don't got to say nothing," Ruben says, interrupt-ing me. "If they don't get me, me and Manuel, we take care of you till you get back to work. We get you any stuff you need — " Manuel keeps his cigarette at the center of his mouth. "You just give us a list."

"I can manage," I say. I am feeling stronger. It is my turn now. "But what will you do, Ruben Fontanez — ? Where will you stay — ?"

"In places," he says. "You gone to see a lot of me, the places I got picked out."

"You cannot hide forever, Ruben."

"I know that, man," he says. He is annoyed. I am reaching him, I know. "I got plans — you don't got to worry. I think it all out." He goes to Manuel and takes the cigarette from him, roughly. He draws in on it once, then returns it. He rubs his hand against the side of his trousers. "Anyway, after a while they stop looking for me — one more spic kid don't mean nothing to them." He points a finger at me. "You be surprised how many guys like me making it in this city — "

I do not mind his finger. I think of Mary Santini, of snow. I see my cowboys in their schoolyard. "But what of school?" I ask. "You said you were listening."

He goes to the window and looks at the rooftops of the buildings across the street. "You don't got to worry. Like

I tell you, I got that planned too. I not so stupid — " I hear someone coming up the stairs. Under my bathrobe I am perspiring. I should eat something solid, I know. I will definitely return to school next week. It is a promise. Manuel sucks on his cigarette. I empty the contents of my teapot and fill it with fresh water. Ruben does not stir. His eyes do not move. His mind is somewhere else.

He does not, I realize, hear the steps. Ah, Ruben, Ruben, you will have to be more careful than this. You cannot dream, Ruben Fontanez. Don't you know that? I turn the flame on high. There is knocking on my door.

Ruben starts. He looks at me and for an instant his eyes are wild with fright. Manuel scans the room, looking for a hiding place. He waits for Ruben's decision. "Say who it is — " Ruben whispers.

"Who is it?" I ask, and I smile, for I know already, from the footsteps.

"It is only me — Nydia. I bring the baby."

I explain to Ruben that Nydia lives in the building. "We can't take no chances," he says. "You tell her we students from your school. We come to see how you getting along — "

I open the door. "But you are — " I say, over my shoulder, and I smile.

Nydia enters, holding the baby in her arms, wrapped in a blue blanket. "This is for you," she says, and puts a pot down on my kitchen table. "I got to make for myself anyway — " She stops when she sees my two monkeys. Her eyes go to the floor. She shuffles backwards. "I sorry," she says. "I didn't know you got people — "

I laugh and explain to her that the two boys are students of mine from the school. She smiles, shyly, but does not look up. "I come get the pot later, when you not busy."

"That your baby?" Ruben asks.

Nydia nods, embarrassed. Ruben whistles. "Man, you pretty young to be having kids — "

"Ruben," I say. "There is no — "

"I'm sorry," he says, and comes toward us. He is not as tall as Nydia, and he too, I realize, is suddenly shy. He tickles the baby under the chin. "Hey, *muchacho,* I got a brother like you — only I not going to see him no more — " He looks at Nydia, briefly. "It's okay if you got a baby."

"I am married," Nydia says. Her eyes are defiant.

"Man, I know that — " Ruben says, and walks away. "What you think — every guy want to make it with you?"

"Ruben — !" I say, and move toward him. Manuel gets up from his crouch. He eyes me carefully.

"Okay, okay," Ruben says. *"Lo siento, lo siento.* You not so beautiful anyway," he adds. "Manuel's sister more beautiful than you — "

Nydia's baby begins to cry and she soothes it. "I see you later, Mister Meyers," she says. "You feeling better?"

"Yes, child," I say. I lift the lid from the pot and steam escapes. Nydia tries to apologize for not giving me something better, but I tell her that I am fond of oatmeal. It is one of my favorites. Ruben comes closer, conscious, I can tell, of every move he makes. Nydia watches him from under her eyelids.

"Your husband got a job?" Ruben asks.

"Yes."

"Okay," Ruben says. "It's okay then."

Manuel's eyes are away from us. We do not concern

him any longer. "I like to speak to you when you get some time," Nydia says to me. "About — you know — school."

I tell her that I will ask the others to leave, but she says no. I promise that I will come down to her apartment later, but she does not like this idea either. She is afraid Carlos will come home, I know, though she says it is because I should not leave my room while I am ill. Ruben says that he will not be staying much longer. He has to go to work also. He looks out the window. He is waiting, he tells us. Soon he will be able to leave.

"Where you live?" he asks.

Nydia looks at me and when I nod, she tells Ruben. "Okay," he says. "I knock on your door when we on our way out — three times, quick — so you know it's okay to come up."

The water for the tea is boiling now and I put leaves in. I ask Nydia if she would like some and she says no. She must clean her apartment. Ruben says he will have some tea. He will need it because of the day he has ahead of him. Nydia's baby is asleep now. She looks at him and her face glows. I touch her elbow and walk her to the door. I thank her for thinking of me. "I think I know what you want to talk to me about," I say. I pat her arm. "I am glad, Nydia." She smiles and leaves, holding her child close to her.

"You got to see Manuel's sister sometime," Ruben says when Nydia is gone.

"You were not very nice," I say to him. "You did not even — "

"I bet you I older than she is," he says. He looks out the window. His face is troubled. There are no trees out there, my monkey. You will see no cowboys. I fix the tea for us and I hum to myself. Perhaps I will sit in the park with Morris this weekend. We will see. I am happy about Nydia's decision.

"That the truth about going to work," Ruben says when I give him his tea. He nods toward Manuel. "That the reason he smoke so much — " Ruben taps Manuel on the head with his knuckles, lightly. "You got to see us in action sometime. You be surprised what we do — "

"I am listening," I say.

"This tea pretty good," he says. He is enjoying himself, I can tell, and that is all right also. His nose in the cup, his eyes laugh at me. "We take you with us sometime — to show you what we do." He licks the edge of his lower lip. His tongue reaches almost to his chin. "When you get better. It be a real treat for you — I give you my promise." He helps himself to a spoonful of sugar and sits down. "Without the money from the welfare I gone to need more for food and things — " Manuel shakes his head. "My good friend Manuel, he want to get me everything I need." Ruben comes closer to me. "I tell you what I think, Mister Meyers. If you got a good friend in this world, you don't need nothing else. That what I think. Manuel, he do anything for me — " He stops and laughs. "Except to die." Manuel smiles. I am certain of it. "That the reason he a true friend. When we first come on the boat together, I think he ready to die for me if I ask him to, but he learn things since then. Like I tell you, he not so C.R.M.D. — " Manuel blows smoke toward the ceiling.

"But we taking enough chances already," he goes on. "And we got to get you the things from your list."

"I can manage," I say. "I have told you. I have friends also, Ruben."

"We get you what you need," he says.

I remind him of Morris. "We have been friends since we were boys," I say. "He brings what I need." I drink my tea and I am watching Morris again, that first time we waited outside the cowboys' Yeshiva. His green wool cap was pulled down over his ears. He was no more than twelve years old then. I laugh because I suddenly remember something: he was smoking. I watch Manuel and continue to laugh. "Since we were boys," I say again. You walked alongside the cowboys, Morris, and I walked behind you. You flaunted them by blowing your smoke into the air around their heads. They were ashamed. Well. Times change, Morris. It is all right. Harry Meyers does not think less of you because you have come to fear them. You are entitled also. Your life has not been easy. I did not know what went on behind the doors of your house in those days. We never know, after all. I wonder what goes on behind the doors of monkeys. All right. Now is not the time to ask such things. When the door is closed, it is closed. Ah, Ruben, Ruben, even if you would try to tell me all, you could not, could you. It is all right. Save your money, my monkey. As for Harry Meyers, in this instance, he can set a good example. The cowboys and the Board of Education have secured his old age for him. What they did to your grandmother will not happen to Harry Meyers, I can assure you. "He brings what I need," I say. "Save your money."

Manuel is tapping on the window with his fingernails. His eyes are wide open. My monkeys have their arms around one another's shoulders. I look to the window. From my angle I can see the top stories of the Hotel Manhattan Towers, on Broadway. The tenements are in front of it, their walls crashed in, their floors used as parking lots. Well. It will not happen on this block. Five-story brownstones do not make good garages. They are too narrow. You are safe from that, Sarah. Ruben is telling Manuel that he was not worried. He knew he would come. I move toward my monkeys. Morris had his arm around my shoulder also. I lift my arms slightly, toward Ruben and Manuel, but I am not ready for such things. The impulse is a momentary one and I restrain it. They are monkeys, after all. "It is Marty!" Ruben says to me. His eyes are bright. He is happy. "There — !"

I follow the direction of his finger and, on the roof of the boarded-up brownstone, number 173, I see the figure of a boy standing at the front edge of the building, his hands on his hips. My eyes move forward. I press my glasses backwards to sharpen the picture. The fronts of his feet are half off the building, his head is bent forward, and he gazes at the street below. I reach toward the window, but Ruben laughs and I lower my hand. "It's okay," he says. "You don't got to be scared for him. He loves it when he goes up high."

Manuel is smoking furiously, his neck craned forward. The boy looks our way and his expression does not seem to change. He points toward the street and our eyes follow. A policeman twirls his nightstick as he walks along. The boy walks from roof to roof. Between numbers 165 and 163 there is a wide space. "*¡Mira!*" Ruben whispers. "*¡Mira!*" He is excited. Marty walks backwards and disappears from view. A moment later he is back. Under his arm he carries a long plank of wood. He lays it across the open space, tests it by bouncing on the end, and then, without even looking our way, he walks across. I clutch the back of Ruben's shirt. "He is our leader," Ruben says. "You gone to like him, Mister Meyers." The boy is directly across from us now. I let go of Ruben's flannel shirt. My palm is wet. The boy is wearing sneakers and his toes curl over the front edge of the building. Something is slung over his shoulder. He watches the policeman and he makes a gesture with his middle finger that causes my monkeys to laugh.

"He gets the guys who build the buildings to let him walk around up high," Ruben says to me. "When you better, we take you around with us, you get to watch Marty work with the steel men." He lifts his head, then waves to Marty. He is very proud. "He the smartest guy I know, Mister Meyers. That the truth." I watch the boy's face, but it is difficult to see him clearly from this distance. My eyes are not focusing well. He wears dungarees and a denim jacket. His head is covered with something black. He seems to be my monkey's age. Fourteen, perhaps fifteen. "Even where I live, they give him respect, Mister Meyers. He know a lot of things." His face is animated. "He lives near here by the river, in a place for the rich people. Me and Manuel, we been working with him since after school starts."

Marty spits toward the street and turns away. My monkey asks if it is all right to have told him where Harry Meyers lives. I say it is and I step back. When I turn, I see that the brightness outside has imposed a ghostly reflection on the inside of my room. I see the rectangle of my window, the shape of the boy on the edge of the roof silhouetted in its frame. They linger above my rug. I hear a hissing sound inside my skull, behind my nose. My eyes tear, my head is heavy. I stumble and catch hold of

the back of a wooden chair. Ruben is beside me at once.
I breathe quickly and he leads me to the bed. Manuel
brings a glass of water.

"It is all right," I say. I drink and the water is cold.
"The sun has made me dizzy. That is all."

Manuel blows his smoke away from me. "Marty be
here in a minute," Ruben says. "He know what medicine
to get. We run down for you."

"It was the sun," I say. "I am all right."

"Maybe you gone to lie down for a while," Ruben says.
He takes my pillow out from under the spread.

I grab at his shoulder and spin him away. "Stop it!"
I command. "I said I am all right." The shouting irritates
my throat. I cough and Ruben moves toward me again.
"Go away," I say. "Go away, Ruben Fontanez." Manuel
is poised behind him, his eyelids drooping. "Go," I say.
"Leave me."

I sit down on the bed. The room turns slowly. I will
have Morris lower the heat. Enough, Harry. Enough.
The buzzer sounds. "Go," I say. "Leave me, Ruben Fontanez."

"But you got to meet Marty," Ruben says. He is holding the doll now and his body before me is misshapen and
blurred. His forehead is huge. He plays with the pins,
but there are no pains in my chest. The cold has settled
in my head. "I tell him all about you." Ruben puts the
doll back on the mantel. "He says he heard about you
anyway. He says people know you because of what you did
on the bulletin board." I lift my head. "He says he seen
you in the neighborhood before. People know you, Mister
Meyers. That the truth —"

It is not so bad to be sick, I think. I can understand

why people go to hospitals. All right, all right, Ruben. The visiting hour is not yet over. If we are lucky, Morris will come before Marty leaves. We can share the sweet roll. I will invite Mrs. Wenger to join us, and the Oriental from upstairs, the two young men who occupy the garden apartment on the ground floor. The garbage-can woman also, if you like. Soon the entire neighborhood will surround my bed, Ruben. Soon. Miss Teitlebaum and Mrs. Davies and Mr. Greenfeld will come also. Danny and Jean and Mary and the policeman. They will read to me of my heroism. I will post a notice at the foot of the staircase with the hours listed. We will have rules and regulations, you see. Carlos will bring his friends. Menachem Schiffenbauer will lead a pilgrimage. The Rebbe will dance around my bed. Morris can invite the men who share his room and we will see if the builders can arrange something for you also, Sarah.

I have heard no steps, but suddenly there is knocking on the door. "I promise you, Mister Meyers. You not gone to be sorry — " I hear the lock move. I put the spread back over the pillow and tuck it in on the sides. Perhaps I will invest in a portable television set so that my cowboys will have something to do when they visit me. They can watch their sporting events and debate with Manuel about batting averages.

"This is my good friend Marty," Ruben is saying. "He is our leader."

A tiny hand is in mine. Its fingers are cold and smooth, the grip is firm. "What's the good word, Meyers?" a voice asks. I look at the boy and his smile is set in the side of his face. Across his top row of teeth is a strip of silver. Across his forehead, around his mouth, his chin, are num-

D

berless blackheads. "I heard about you too," he says, from the side of his face. He pumps my hand some more. "I respect a guy like you, Meyers." He releases my hand, pats me on the shoulder, then turns to Manuel. "You got a butt for me, Manny my boy?" he asks.

Manuel gives him a cigarette. My new visitor closes his eyes when he inhales and the smoke drifts from the corners of his thin mouth. He is no taller than my two monkeys and when he opens his eyes and stares at me I must close my own. His eyes, of course, are the eyes of a cowboy. I am not surprised. It is no use. Resign yourself, Harry. Soon. They will all be here. Visiting hours will be without end. I look at him as he paces around the room. A green canvas bookbag hangs over his left shoulder. On the side of his head is a black beret. His face is round, his nose large, his movements silent and graceful despite the fact that he is heavy. Perhaps, I think, perhaps you too have been hanging in trees this morning, Marty, and dancing across lawns. Your beret is covering your beard. You cannot fool Harry Meyers.

"Sit down, sit down," he is saying to me. "Ruben tells me you've been sick, so I don't want you playing host to me, right?" He brushes his hair from his forehead and when I see him shove the ends under his beret I remember Morris in his green wool hat. He is laughing and talking to me. "He made one of you too, huh?" he says. I nod. He holds it next to my face. "Ruben baby," he says. "I got to hand it to you — you've got the talent. Right, Meyers?"

I nod.

"One of your best, one of your best," Marty says as he places my likeness back on the fireplace mantel. Ruben informs Marty that when I am better he has offered to take me to see them in action. He wonders if he has done the right thing. Marty stands in front of me, his two assistants behind him. I smile at him, but in truth, my stomach is very weak. I taste something sour. Now that there is no telephone service, perhaps it will speed the arrival of Jackson's brother. It will be best, after all, if things are accomplished quickly. "I respect a guy like you, Meyers," Marty says. "I want you to know that." I see Ruben's eyes, smiling shyly. "I mean it. The way you handle the kids in Ruben's school — what you did in the park — " He clicks his tongue. "So what I've been thinking is this: if you want, when you retire at the end of the year, maybe we can find a place for you in our outfit." His hand is on my shoulder, monkey eyes glistening behind him. "You don't have to say yes or no. Think it over, right? Wait till you get a chance to see us operate, and if — "

I nod. There is silence. Then he is laughing at my puzzled expression. His arms are around the shoulders of his two monkeys. "Ah, I'm just putting you on, Meyers — don't mind me." He swings the canvas bag and it falls on the bed next to me. "What's the good word, Ruben baby?" he asks. "You give the slip to that joker from the city yet?"

Ruben tells Marty about his escape in the cemetery and Marty praises him. Manuel edges his way between the two of them and whispers something in Marty's ear. "It is true," Ruben says. Marty pounds Manuel on the back. "Manny, you're the most!" he says. They go to the window together, talking and giggling and then Marty returns. "Listen," he says. His tone is confidential. "I don't like to butt into anybody's business, but you ought to do something about that guy Greenfeld at your school, Meyers." He sits down next to me. "Put him wise, man, or one of these first days he's not gonna look so pretty." He wipes his mouth with the back of his hand, points at Manuel, and laughs. His laugh is gentle, a boy's laugh. I do not mind it. "That Manny!" he says, shaking his head. "You know what he did yesterday?" He leans against me, his hand cupped over his mouth. "What he's been promising: he gave Greenfeld a good kick in the nuts." He sucks on his lower lip. "Bam!" he says, socking his fist into the palm of his hand. "Right in the old bazoojies!" He moves away again. "I only wish I'd been there, Manny my boy," he says, and Manuel shuffles at Marty's heels, his eyes wide open, his mouth sucking on a fresh cigarette. Ruben stands by the fireplace.

"I'm telling you something, Meyers," Marty whispers to me. "If this Greenfeld is a friend of yours, put him wise, man." He leans close to me and for an instant my nose clears. I see his braces and smell his breath as it comes toward me. It is sweet. He puts his hand on my shoulder. "Listen to me: Manny's a born killer," he whispers. "I'm telling you something, Meyers. Man to man and I'm not putting you on about this. I can tell." He looks around. "A born killer."

"Mr. Greenfeld is no friend of mine," I say.

"Okay, okay," Marty says, irritated. "But I'm speaking straight to you — I know Manny, what makes him tick. He'll kill the guy one of these first days, marine or no marine. You mark my word."

"Mr. Greenfeld is no marine."

"That's what I said: marine or no marine." His grip

on my shoulder tightens. "Manny's no C.R.M.D., Meyers — I'm giving it to you straight, right? If he — "

I rip his hand from my shoulder. "Stop!" I say. "Get out! Out!" I shove against his chest and he slides from my view. My monkeys draw near. "Stop!" I cry, and I am on my feet. My fists are raised and all around me I can feel the cold and the snow. "Stop." I am taller than my three adversaries. "Get out, get out — " I see Marty's silhouette as he stands on top of the brownstones across the street. I will get him a longer plank of wood. Then he can cross 76th Street from one side to the other without walking up and down so many flights. It is the least I can do. "All right," I say. Do not expect the garbage-can woman to notice you, though, my friend. All right. Have it your way. It is nothing to me. I tell them other things as well. Things that are on my mind. When I am done I let myself rest on the bed. I am entitled. There is no need to pretend about my health. I do not need to wait for the end of visiting hours. Harry Meyers can rest if he wants to. Danny will protect me.

Marty barks orders and there is water at my lips, in Manuel's hands. Ruben is behind me on the bed, sitting on his haunches, rubbing my shoulders at either side of my neck. Marty has removed my eyeglasses and, with his thumb and forefingers, he applies pressure at the bridge of my nose, pressing against the inner edge of my eye sockets. I do not struggle. He takes his hands away and I feel an easing of the tension that is truly wonderful. He repeats the procedure. I sigh, then cough lightly, clearing my throat. "Take it easy," Marty is saying to me. "Just relax." I breathe deeply and the room shifts. I lean to one side but Marty straightens me. "Okay, okay," he says and takes something from the pocket of his jacket. "Take a whiff of this —"

He passes something green in front of my nose. I sniff and my nostrils quiver. My eyes smart. "Better?" he asks.

"It is only a cold," I say.

"Sure, sure," he says. His face is in front of mine and when he lowers the lid of my right eye and looks in, I do not fight him. "He's talking straight," Marty says to his monkeys. "It's only a cold. But you need to rest, Meyers. Plenty of sleep, lots of fluid and you'll be as good as new." He goes to the refrigerator and opens it. Then he inspects my cabinet. He wets the end of a pencil with his tongue and writes on a piece of paper. The paper is given to Manuel. "Be careful," Ruben says. The door opens and closes.

Marty tells me to get under the covers and I do what he says. The sheets are cool, but I do not forget the warmth of your thighs, Sarah. I wink at Ruben and he smiles. There is no need to tell him of the dream. Marty sits down across from me, in my easy chair, from where he can command a view of the street. I am certain he is the equal of my cowboys in cunning. He tells me to close my eyes and I do. The room is warmer now and I pull the covers tight under my chin. I apologize to them for not having shaved. Ruben tells me that Marty will never have to shave. Marty ignores him. It is nothing to me. "I telling you the truth, Mister Meyers," Ruben says. I believe you, my monkey. I look at Marty. So, I think, it is as I thought: you are a beardless cowboy, a pale monkey. "Show him your spots," Ruben says.

"After Manny gets back with the goods, we're gonna have to split out," Marty says. He exhales. "Now that he gave it to Greenfeld, all three of us are on the lam — "

"Show him your spots," Ruben says again, but Marty continues to ignore him. He tells me that it is too bad that I do not have a hole in the septum of my nose, for if I did he could tie a twig of baywood there and within twenty-four hours my cold would be gone. It is guaranteed. I do not doubt his word. After all, Ruben claims that he will never have to shave. And he has spots. I hum to myself. *Whistle while you work* . . . I feel my mattress bend and I know that Ruben is beside me. "You got to tell him to show you the spots." Ruben says to me. "Please, Mister Meyers — " I raise my eyelids. Ah, Ruben, Ruben. Harry Meyers does not make the same mistake twice. I will keep my hands under the covers, believe me. I breathe through my mouth. "It's why he don't got to shave."

"Cool it, Ruben," Marty says. "Let the guy get some shut-eye."

"On his back," Ruben whispers to me.

That is all. Marty yanks my monkey from the bed. I open my eyes and watch Ruben dance around Marty, feinting with his hands. There is a swishing sound, a thud, and my monkey is on the floor, his leader on top of him, twisting his arm upwards in the small of his back. Ruben winces. "Tell him, Mister Meyers. Please — the spots!" Marty applies more pressure and I fear for my monkey's arm. "Tell him," Ruben says. All right, I think. Enough. "All right," I say. "The spots — "

"Ah," Marty says, and he releases Ruben at once. "Dirty pool, Ruben baby. Dirty pool." He steps across my monkey and sneers at him. *"Su madre — "* he begins, but Ruben is happy, I see. His expression is triumphant.

I sit up, leaning on one elbow. Marty is talking. "Okay?"
He stands in front of me, bent over, his jacket and shirt
jerked up over his head. His back is pink and young.
Ruben claps his hands and stands beside him. *"¡Mira!"*
he exclaims. *"¡Mira!"*

"Okay?" Marty asks, again. "I can't stay like this all
day — "

I shake the sleep from my head and lean closer.
"¡Mira!" Ruben whispers and he points a bony finger to
the lower region of Marty's back, where, along the right
side of his spine I see what Ruben has been referring to.
"¡Morado!" Ruben says, breathless. I shrug, at first, thinking they are ordinary birthmarks. *"¡Morado!"* I look
more closely and see that my monkey is correct. The
spots are not the usual brown, but a dull shade of purple.

"Yes," I say. "All right." Marty moves away from us
and tucks his shirt in quickly. He is annoyed.

"He does not like to show them — " Ruben says. "So
I got to thank you, Mister Meyers. It is not every — "

"Cool it, Ruben," Marty says. "I showed the spots, right?
Now just cool it — "

"But — " I begin.

"¡Morado! Ah ¡morado!" My monkey is in a trance.
"Ah *morado* — "

Marty grabs him from behind with one hand, squeezing
his neck. He knows the pressure points also. "How many
times I got to tell you something?" He shoves Ruben
away, but my monkey still smiles. His eyes are glazed.

"But — " I begin.

"Look," Marty says, approaching my bed. "They're just
Mongolian spots, see? They're not so unusual."

"The Indians come from Mongolia," Ruben whispers.

"Marty has taught us. They crossed from Siberia. They too were hairless — "

"Cool it, Ruben," Marty says. "I told you — "

"The spots do not lie, Mister Meyers," Ruben says. "Señora Rosa — "

"Señora Rosa eats it," Marty says. He raises a hand and Ruben retreats to the fireplace. He takes the packet of earth from his pocket but Marty sneers at him. All right. I will leave my Persian slippers for Manuel. It is decided. And my bedspread for Nydia. Ruben stands by the window now, fondling my likeness, playing with the pins. After all, I think, he is only a boy. I was right the first time. "Listen," Marty is saying. He is next to me now and he speaks so that Ruben cannot hear. "Man to man, what do you think — ? Just because I got the spots and I don't have much hair yet, I think I'm an Indian?" He laughs to himself and clicks his tongue. His hand is on my knee. "I'm not that far gone, Meyers. Right? Not yet. Maybe my old man could sell those doctors a bill of goods. Sure. With all his money, you think they were gonna — "

"But I — "

He is angered by my interruption. He stands over me now and commands me to look at him. He unbuttons his shirt and pulls up his undershirt. "Okay?" he says. "You get a good look?" I nod. He rolls up his trousers and shows me his legs. Ruben's eyes dance wildly. "¡Mira! ¡Mira!" he says, breathless. "Now I'm showing you this once and for all, Meyers, and that's it, right? You got questions, you fire away now. It's the only chance you'll get, you hear?"

I shrug. "I am an old man," I say.

Marty smiles from the side of his face. He pats me on

the shoulder and speaks confidently again. "Look," he is saying, "so I'm not straight and narrow like my older brothers, right? So I got these spots. And no hair yet, right? So what am I supposed to do, let people use it against me?" He taps the side of his head with his forefinger. "That's what they'd like, I'll tell you that. But you won't get me to suck around my old man the way they do. With all his money I still showed him, you hear?" He moves his head up and down. "They won't get me." His grip on my knee is firm. I enjoy the sound of his voice. It has an edge to it. It comes from his throat. "They won't get me, you understand?"

I shrug. Sarah would comfort you, my young rebel.

"Okay, okay," he says. My silence bothers him. "You want to hear the whole thing, don't you? You want it spelled out, black and white, right?" He stops and his eyes rivet on mine. They are gray, I see. But what color are my monkey's eyes, I wonder. I cannot recall. I can see him clearly — when he danced on the desk, in the street below his home — and I can see his eyes flashing. Yet I cannot recall their color. "You and me, Meyers, we understand one another, right?" I nod. "You have spots," I say, and I try to smile. Marty winks. "Okay," he says, so that Ruben can hear. He lowers his voice again and talks to me like a true friend. We will share his secret. "Okay," he is saying. "So I say to myself — Marty, what are you gonna do about it? Right? And you know what the answer is — "

I look at him. "Compensate," he says. He laughs again. "I turn it into an asset, see?" He glances toward Ruben. "Like keeping my men in line — you know what I mean? Giving them all that Indian stuff — "

"The spots do not lie," Ruben says. He is closer to us, holding his doll, and I wonder if he has heard everything Marty has been saying. As for me, I would prefer it. There should be no secrets.

"Listen to me, Meyers," Marty says. There is urgency in his voice. "I'm shooting straight with you. I showed my old man and I can show you — "

I smile. His threats do not disturb me. "He knows everything about the Indians," Ruben says. "Ask him — "

"Sure, Ruben baby. Sure," he says, and winks at me. "See what I mean? Where I want 'em. See — ?"

Marty moves away from the bed without waiting for a response from me. In the middle of the room he turns and points a finger in my direction. "You want to believe it, you believe it. You don't, don't. It's no skin off my ass — "

I nod. "Of course," I say. But I know that Harry Meyers disturbs him. He looks out the window and chews on his lip. I had a scheme once also, Marty, and I spent many nights drawing up the proposal. Sarah encouraged me. "There's Manny," Marty says. "He's got the goods — "

Marty turns sideways and the light from the window catches his silver brace and flashes at me. "Look," he says. "Just cool it, both of you." He does not look at us. "You, Meyers, I told the story once, I'm not explaining again. I don't make a practice of repeating myself, you hear?" The buzzer sounds and I start to get up, but Ruben presses the button at the side of the door. If the Board of Education had accepted the plan, my monkey, you and your brothers would have grown up on farms. You might have qualified also, Marty. Get them away from the homes, I explained. Tear down the schools. Use the money to buy land upstate. Build work-farms. Sarah smiled. I had energy then. Like you, Marty. "Okay. Wait outside," he says to Ruben. He is pacing now, nervous. "I got to straighten something out."

Ruben obeys. But you did not wait long enough, Sarah. And Harry Meyers was doing it more to please you than because he cared. That seems to be the truth. I showed a draft to a school supervisor I knew. He was sympathetic, but he let me know how unoriginal my plan was. And he reminded me of the obstacles that waited at Livingston Street, the technicalities, the endurance I would need to get even a hearing. It was only a dream, Sarah. I wonder if I ever thought otherwise. From his canvas bag, Marty takes out a pair of drums. "They're bongos." He laughs, but his laugh is forced. "Ruben and Manny call them my tom-toms." I do not smile. I hear whispering outside the door. Marty looks at me. "Look," he says. "I want to settle this once and for all, Meyers, you understand?" He sits on my bed. "I mean, man to man, who knows why or when I got hooked on this Indian bit, right? But I did." He licks his lips. "And I'll tell you something else — I know all the theories, too, you hear?"

"I do not understand — " I say.

"C'mon, c'mon — " he says. "Sure you do. Don't make out like you're innocent. You don't fool me. Ruben told you all about me already, right? About why I'm on the lam — " He does not wait for an answer. He would surely have been a leader at the farm. "But the theories don't matter. So long as I cope, right? And I cope in this world, Meyers. I'll tell you that. They won't get me, you hear?"

"Of course," I say.

The door is open and Marty's arms are around the

shoulders of his two monkeys. "Compensate, man. Compensate." They walk before me. "Jesus," he says. "At twenty-five smackers a session, you know how we could be living now, Ruben baby? In style, man. Style —"

"We making it," Ruben says.

Marty takes the grocery bag from Manuel and he and Ruben empty its contents on my kitchen table. I count six large cans. "Good boy, Manny," Marty says. "I didn't know what your favorite was, so we got you a selection — apricot, pineapple, orange, grapefruit — two each of the apricot and orange, okay?"

"I will pay you," I say.

Marty laughs. "Manny knows the owner," he says. "It's for good will, right, Manny my boy?"

Manuel takes a package of cigarettes from his side pocket, then a paper bag from under his shirt.

"And use this," Marty says, handing me a small plastic container. I read the label. It is Triaminicin, a nasal decongestant. "Most of this junk is for the birds — and the prices are way out of line — but it relieves symptoms. You can't get any good stuff unless you have a prescription." I sit up straight and press the sides of the plastic bottle, spraying into each nostril. "Okay — now lie back down," Marty says.

Manuel places a full glass of juice on my night table. I look at it. From its color I can tell that it is apricot nectar. My favorite. I will give some to Morris. He will share the oatmeal with me also. I taste the medicine as it drips down at the back of my throat.

"I gone to bring you something else," Ruben says. "When we come back. It be a surprise —" Manuel is careful to blow the smoke away from me.

"Your head should begin to clear in about five to ten minutes," Marty says. "You rest up now and you'll be okay." He pauses. "If you're not, you don't have to pay us, right?" He explains then to his two monkeys that the Indian custom of paying the medicine man only if he cures the patient, was, of course, derived from the Chinese custom. He winks at me. Not all the tribes practiced it, he says. Ruben says it was the same with Señora Rosa. I sit up and drink the juice. It is thick and soothing. It is all right if I doze. Morris will be buzzing me soon. Nydia will come to confer. "If you think of anything else you need, you just write it down," Marty says. "Then leave the rest to Manny."

Ruben leans my doll against the lamp, on my night table, beside the juice glass. I do not mind. It pleases him that I have kept it, I know. And the pains in my chest are almost gone. My glands will be down in a day or two, I am certain. Then I will return. Ruben leans close to me. "Manuel's sister say she like me," he says. "She waiting for us downstairs, to go to work — "

I smile. I feel very drowsy, peaceful. Ruben, you will not even need to storm the hospitals. With your charm, you will get past the policemen with ease. Marty will work from the rooftops. I reach for my eyeglasses, on the night table. I will see what color your eyes are, my monkey. "We'll split now," Marty is saying. "You rest up. When we get back from work, we'll stop by. Okay?"

"I bring you a surprise," Ruben says. The door opens. "I see you later. We gone to make our money now."

The door locks automatically. I am not afraid to dream this time. It will be all right. My three young men are going to work. I drink some more juice and hum to myself. Already my nose has stopped dripping. I will sleep until Morris comes, then I will talk with Nydia. By next Monday I will return to school. Before then, if my health continues to improve, I will take up Ruben's offer.

When my nose clears, I shift onto my side. Then I turn to my stomach. It is dark. The shades are pulled down and I cannot see the brownstones across the street. I will look into my monkey's eyes when he returns. It is too late now. I hear the children singing. Their voices are pleasant and soft. *Whistle while you work . . . Hitler is a jerk . . . Mussolini is a meanie . . .*

FIVE

I HEAR a swishing sound. My body is in a sweat, the covers are heavy, my pajamas stick to me. Underneath, the sheets are warm and damp. Someone has laid another blanket on top of me. I do not move. I cannot remember the last time my sleep was so black and dreamless. I do not mind, though. I have had enough cowboys in trees, enough dolls, enough even of you, Sarah. You never did answer my question about your extra years, you know.

I breathe in. My sinuses are clear. Sarah, Sarah. It is all right. I don't hold it against you, believe me. The swishing continues. I lie half on my side, half on my stomach, my arms locked around the pillow. I can hear the Rebbe singing. My eyes are terribly thick. It seems a shame to open them. Perhaps my monkeys have returned. Morris should have been here long ago, unless my sleep has been more brief than I can realize. There is no way of knowing, after all. I reach my hand across and touch the juice glass, then my eyeglasses.

The room is still dark. The window shades are drawn, but I can see my likeness smiling at me. In a corner of the room the swishing persists. I swallow and feel the lumps slide along the underside of my jaw. A shape moves. I pull the chain of my lamp and the sound stops. The shape is that of a woman, I see. She moves silently across the room and I watch her dark outline. She carries a long pole.

"Sarah — "

"It only me, Mister Meyers," she says. "Nydia — "

I nod. "It is all right, child," I say. On the farm, the girls would have lived separately. There would have been useful work for them. I had plans.

"Here," she says, and pours juice into my glass. "The boy say to give it to you when you wake up." The mop rests against the railing at the foot of my bed. There is a white pill next to the juice glass and I put it on my tongue. Nydia sits across from me now, by the fireplace. I drink and the liquid soothes my throat. I slip a finger behind my glasses and wipe the sleep from the inner edge of my eye. The light from my lamp makes a circle on the floor and leaves Nydia's face in shadows. I see only her legs, her sandals, the gray wool skirt that falls across her knees.

"I clean your kitchen for you," she offers.

"The baby?"

"I leave him downstairs. My mother come to watch him while Carlos at work — "

I drink more juice. Nydia gets up. Her body moves smoothly across the room. She raises the window shades and I see that it is already dark outside. I look for Marty on the rooftops but I see only television antennas.

"I talk with my mother about what I gone to ask you. She know that you a teacher." I see her face now. She looks at the floor. "If Carlos find out I want to go to night school he get angry and — " She stops. " — and do things."

She hesitates. On my night table my doll is smiling at me. "Did you want to ask me something?" I say.

She is surprised by my response. "I thought — " she begins. I sit up and find that I am somewhat dizzy. I can hear the sound of my voice and I know why Nydia takes a step backwards. "I think maybe you could help me get ready," she says. "I not been in school since — "

I nod, cutting her off, but I do not say anything. Beyond the edge of my rug, under the windows, I can see the linoleum drying where Nydia has been working. I picture her mother, rocking the baby in her arms by the window, watching the street. "If you don't got the time — "

"What about Carlos?" I ask.

She shrugs. "My mother says she come to watch the baby. And Carlos be working nights soon, to make the extra money." I watch her fingers turn slowly in her lap, and my mind turns with them. "My mother say she give you the money, and I come to clean and cook for you when — "

"Stop," I say. "Enough. I will think about it. Stop now. All right?"

She nods. My head does not clear. "A man was here," she says.

"A man?"

"While you sleep." She is uncomfortable. I can see my monkey walking around her, surveying her young body. "A big man — he say he be back."

"A colored man?"

"No."

"It was Morris," I say. "We were boys together."

"I guess I go now." She moves to the door. "I sorry to bother you — "

Above the brownstones the sky is a deep blue. I lift the covers and put on my slippers, then my robe. I will look at your eyes later, my monkey. "I would like to meet your mother sometime," I say.

Nydia smiles. "You like her," she says. "You like Carlos also," she adds quickly. She steps toward me. Between her skirt and sweater I see a narrow strip of brown skin. "When you know him sometime. You see — "

"I am sure," I say.

"I worry about him sometime, but I afraid to tell my mother. She say she gone to call the police on him next time — " I wander away from her and see that she has cleaned the grease from my gas burners.

"Would you like some juice?" I ask.

She shakes her head. "I like to talk to you sometime, Mister Meyers," she says. "I got to tell *some*body about what he do when he get crazy in the head — "

"I am an old man," I say, and I smile at her.

"Your boys from the school, they look up to you." I drink more juice and wonder when my monkeys will return. "Carlos, when he not happy, he do things — "

"What?" I ask. The question is out, abruptly, and I am not unhappy about it. It is the least I can do in return for her services. "What does he do?"

She moves her shoulders. Her neck is lovely. The shadow from the mop handle rises on the wall. "To the cat we used to have — he — he do a bad thing."

"Yes?"

She shivers and crosses her arms upon her bosom, holding herself. "I tell my mother the cat run away, but — "

"And you would like me to help you with your studies?"

She is confused momentarily. She nods. She comes toward me and I move away so that she cannot touch me with her young fingers. I know these games. "Sometimes Carlos, he come home late at night from drinking with his friends and he say things to me — in *El Barrio* he say he see me with other men — he call the baby ugly — ! I — "

The buzzer sounds. I smile. It is on time, I think. Marty has scheduled things perfectly. Nydia moves to the kitchen table and puts her cleaning rags in a paper bag. "I — I sorry," she says.

"Sorry?"

"I got to tell somebody." Her eyes are wide now and they are not the eyes of a young girl. "He a very good husband sometimes, Mister Meyers. You got to believe me! That why I like to go to school again, so I can — "

She sees that I am not interested. The buzzer sounds again. I go to the door and press the button. I look at my young student and know that she will not receive her answer from Harry Meyers today. I am sorry also. But there are other things to think about, Nydia. I hear steps. She seems frightened. She does not, I realize, want to see my three guardians again today. She runs her tongue over her lips and her eyes seem tired suddenly. "What," I ask her, "did Carlos do to your cat?"

She grabs the doorknob. A knocking comes at once from the other side and she backs away. I will not look into your eyes, my child. I hear the door open. A man is standing there, tall and broad-shouldered. As Nydia slides by him, I start to follow her. There was no need for the

question, after all. "Hey, what are you doin' out of bed?"
The door closes and I let Danny push me backwards into
the room. In his right hand he is carrying a large leather
suitcase. A bag of groceries is cradled in the nook of his
left arm. He wears a black overcoat. "C'mon, Mister
Meyers, into bed with you." I smell beer on his breath.
"You ain't lookin' so good, you know." He has put his
suitcase down. The groceries are on the kitchen table.
"Boy — cold as a witch's tit out there tonight. They say
it's gonna snow before morning." He takes his coat off
and places it on the easy chair by the fireplace. Then he
pulls the chair from my desk to the bed, and straddles it,
backwards.

"So how ya been feelin'?" he asks.

"It is only a cold," I say.

"Sure," he says. "Sure. That's how come ya look the
way you do, huh?" He shakes his head sideways. I remember what I thought when I viewed my reflection in
the window. I do not fool myself about such things, I can
assure you. He is laughing to himself now, his stomach
knocking against the chair. "I got to hand it to you,
though — sick or not, you don't let up, do you?"

I try to smile at him.

"I knew you had something going for you — " He nods
his head a few times and I see that the hair at the front of
his skull is beginning to thin. The long black strands do
not deceive me. He gestures toward the door with his
head. "Not bad, either, what I seen. At least she cares
about you, you know what I mean? That's something in
a woman nowadays." He bends his head closer to mine.
"But don't you think you ought to go a little easy now — I
mean, your condition and all — ?"

I shrug. "It is only a cold," I say.

He slaps his knee with his right hand. "You're really something, Mister Meyers, I gotta hand it to you." He will not stop wagging his head. "You got some spirit. I was saying that to Jean this afternoon after I come by here. I only hope to God I got your spirit when I'm your age, Mister Meyers." He pats his stomach. "I'll have to get rid of this, though, if I want to keep at it, I guess — huh?" He laughs. "Like that sergeant I was tellin' you about in the army, you remember — ?" I nod. "He said he'd be getting his nooky when he was past seventy, and I believe him. He used to brag to all the younger guys that he was gonna die in the saddle, like that actor did — what was his name — ?" He takes a wrinkled handkerchief from his back pocket and rubs his face with it. "Nice and warm in here," he says. "I'll tell you the truth, if you gotta go, that's the way I'd like to do it." He points a finger at me. "But no sense speeding things up, the way I see it, you know what I mean? You're just gettin' to where you're gonna be able to have all the time in the world — you gotta take care of yourself, Mister Meyers." He puts the back of his fat hand to my forehead and concentrates. "And we're gonna see that you do, hear?"

I nod.

He stands up and paces around the room. He is not happy with the results of his examination. "You want some supper?" he asks.

"No," I say. "I am not hungry. Something to drink would be nice, though."

"Right," he says, and goes to the refrigerator. He is worried about me. I touch my own hand to my forehead. It is warmer than I expected. "I saw from before that you're stocked up pretty good on juice. That's the best thing for you when you got a bad cold." He punctures the top of a can with an opener and rinses out a glass for me. It is grapefruit juice this time and as it goes down it burns slightly. Danny opens a can of beer he has brought for himself and drinks from it, his elbow on the fireplace mantel. "You know something — ? It's not bad here for a one-room place, but Jeannie and I were thinking a man like you, with your education, you ought to have more room for books and things — and a separate kitchen." He tells me that he remembers the apartment on Eastern Parkway, before I moved, when the photographers took pictures of us together. He recognizes the rug in the middle of the floor as one I have brought with me from Brooklyn. It is a rectangular Persian rug and I realize that I have not actually looked at it for years. The birds and trees and flowers that run across it have faded long ago. The dull red color does not interest me. If he admires my room now, think what his feelings will be when I have put the pictures on the walls. He will not see any need for moving then. "What got us worried, see, was when Jean called this morning and found your phone had been disconnected. She called me at work to tell me and first thing I did was to call your school. They told me about you being sick for over a week, so I just said to my foreman — 'Jack, I got something important, you want to reprimand me, go ahead — I don't give a damn — ' and I left the factory and come straight here by cab." He wipes some beer from his chin. I drink my juice. "I told him it was on account of you, and he said he'd cover for me. All the guys at the factory know about you — "

"Of course," I say.

He seems unsure of something. He is considering. Well. He is entitled also, I think. "You were sleeping like a baby when I come here this afternoon — the girl, she says you didn't even budge when I rung the bell. Then when I found — " He puts his beer can down on the table and sits next to me again. In truth, though I am somewhat groggy, I do not feel sick at all. My chest is full and warm. "Well, I just took a cab straight back to Brooklyn and packed up some things. Pajamas and a shirt for tomorrow. I probably forgot something, but I can call and Mary can bring it if I need anything — "

Next year, I think, I will do translations. From Spanish to Hebrew, Hebrew to Spanish. Despite his sidelocks, Menachem Schiffenbauer will be no match for me, I promise you. My cowboys will love the Don and Sancho in Hebrew. Danny's eyes are olive-green, I see. I picture him in a cowboy's hat, with a beard. His nose would be appropriate. But he will have to do away with his stomach. He is right about that. "I figure I can sack out on the easy chair — you know me: give me a couple of beers, I can sleep anywhere. It's wine that keeps me awake — funny, huh? With most people it's the opposite — "

"There is no need," I say. "Go home to your wife and family. It is only a cold — "

"Sure," he says again. He takes a piece of paper from his shirt pocket. "You feelin' better — ?" I nod. "Cause I want to talk to you about somethin' serious. Okay?"

"Of course," I say. Under the covers I clasp my hands on my chest. I slide my fingers from knuckle to knuckle, and along my forearms. Despite the winter, my skin is smooth and soft.

"I mean, I don't like the idea of scolding you like I was

your old man or something, but I feel I gotta lay it on the line with you, Mister Meyers." He looks at the paper, then at me. He cares, truly. I will put him in charge of the others. If he does not like Marty's schedule, he is free to revise it. "The way I figure it, you gettin' sick now — seeing as how you'll be well in a couple of days — it's a lucky break. Otherwise we might never of found out." He smiles. "We know you mean well, Mister Meyers, and you want to spare us and all that — but in the end, if something would happen to you, you'd only cause us more grief. You done enough for us already." He sits up straight. He has finished his deliberations. He wrinkles his brow and is ready to tell me his secret. He does not look directly at me, but I can see that there is something fierce in his eyes. "You should of told me about Jackson's son-of-a-bitch brother," he says. He curses under his breath, in Italian. It is a language I do not know. Perhaps I will study it next year. "He must really be keeping a close tab on you — cause by the time I got here this afternoon, he knew about your phone. It said so in the note. The girl said she found it slipped under the door. She thought some kids from the neighborhood must of done it, so I didn't tell her different." He stops and looks at me. "You been getting a lot of these, right — ?"

"I suppose," I say.

His eyes bulge forward. He leans close to me and whispers. "Well, let him come, baby. Just let him come, Mister Meyers." He motions to his suitcase. "He'll have a surprise in store for him if he comes into this room." He slams his fist into his palm. "A real surprise."

"I suppose," I say.

"And I'll tell you something else — I don't want any

secrets anymore, see — maybe I shouldn't of done it, maybe I should of put the whole thing to you first — but I found all the other notes in your desk." He is embarrassed by this disclosure. "The guy's a real scribbler, ain't he?" he adds.

"People on welfare do not have telephones," I say. "That is the way the city improves their literacy. They must send their messages through the mails, or — "

Danny bursts into laughter. "What a guy!" he says. He slaps his thigh. "I got to remember that for Jeannie." He stops abruptly. He sets his jaw and gives his head a quick jerk. He is not angry with me, I see. My remarks touch him. His admiration for Harry Meyers only increases. "You really got some spirit, don't you?" He is considering again. "Let me tell you something, Mister Meyers, and I hope you don't take it the wrong way — but a lot of guys I work with at the factory, when we get into talks sometimes they say how maybe the Jews all got it from the Nazis cause they had no guts, and I tell 'em they'd think different if they knew a man like you." He pauses. There are extra bed sheets in the bottom drawer of my dresser. He will be able to use those. But all my blankets are on my bed now and I know he will not permit me to give one of them up. "I never seen any point in tellin' you about this before, but now it seems right, you know what I mean?" I nod. Perhaps Manuel can obtain a folding cot. We will see. Marty can take care of himself, I know. I do not worry about him. "Last year, when we were talkin' this way I about broke a guy's jaw for saying that maybe the Nazis had the right idea — " I look into his large face and see, from his eyes, that he is truly moved by the recounting of his own deed. He swallows and I watch his

Adam's apple slide in his throat. "Anyway, I just wanted you to know." His eyes narrow. "You don't hear any of that kind of talk around me anymore. They watch out for Danny Santini — "

"I am sure," I say. Perhaps he will use the bedspread. It is at the foot of my bed now. I can wear woolen socks. He puts the note back into his shirt pocket. If it gives him pleasure to protect me in this way, I think, it is the least I can do for him.

"I'll tell you the truth," he says. "We don't got to worry much till Jackson himself gets sprung. I don't think the kid will do anything on his own, but I figure for a day or two — so long as he knows you're laid up, we better be careful just the same, you know what I mean? We just got to be sure there's somebody here with you all the time." He stops. "You sure you don't want somethin' to eat? I brought some stuff for sandwiches. Cold cuts — or I can warm up some soup."

"A sandwich would be nice," I say. This pleases him. He goes to work at once, and fixes me corned beef on rye. My father, I remember, loved the end pieces of rye bread. His brother, my uncle Nathan, was a baker in the Bialy- stoker Bakery on East Broadway. When he visited us he would always bring a paper bag full of end pieces which my father would warm in the oven. "But if that bastard makes a mistake and comes again while I'm here," Danny says, "I'll do to him just what he promises he's gonna do to you. You can count on it, Mister Meyers." I sit up and rest the plate and sandwich on my lap. The rye bread is fresh. I do not doubt Danny's word. "I got the stuff, and I been waiting a long time —" I did not realize how hungry I was. He has made a sandwich for himself, also, and we eat together while he talks of his plans for Jackson's brother, and for Jackson himself. When I am finished I lie down again. He puts the dishes in the sink and stretches his arms above his head. "Ah, I'm talking too much, huh? I bet you want to get some shut-eye, don't you?" He and Marty will get along, I think, if only they can agree upon who will be in charge. "You look real tired, you know."

"There are sheets in the bottom drawer of the dresser — " I begin, but he interrupts me and says he has a woolen bathrobe which will do. He will prop his feet up on my desk chair. The easy chair, he has discovered, is soft. He can sleep anywhere when he has had some beer, he reminds me. He begins to undress. He remembers something and laughs.

"Hey," he says. "That girl that was up here before — "

"Nydia," I say.

"Yeah." He sucks on his lower lip. *"Marón!"* he says, wagging his hand. "What a piece. You got to hand it to those spics — their young girls are real lookers — "

"She is fifteen years old," I say. "But they will not let her go to school because of the baby."

"Serves her right," he says. "Getting knocked up like — "

"She is married," I say. "If she were not, despite the child, she would be allowed to go to school."

"Yeah," he says. "That's what I mean. These people got no sense about things." He stops then. Something in my tone of voice has disturbed him. "I didn't mean nothing bad about her, using that language — " he says.

"It is all right," I say. "I will visit her when I am better. She wants to speak with me about going to night school."

"Yeah?" He sets his suitcase across the arms of the easy chair and opens it. His pajamas are striped, blue and white. "I give her credit then," he says. He loosens his belt and lets his pants fall to the floor. He wears jockey-style underpants. His thighs are larger than I had imagined. Everywhere, he is full of hair. He chuckles to himself. "I got to hand it to you, though — "

In the hallway I hear the toilet and it reminds me of my own needs. I wonder if, like my students, I will be required to take a pass with me when I leave the room. The thought amuses me. I wonder too if my monkeys miss me. Well. It is not something I have ever given much thought to, but, in truth, I think the answer is that I do not enjoy teaching. I will be glad when it is over. Next year I will do translations. If my monkeys and cowboys miss me, that is their problem. Within three years there will be a new generation of monkeys in Junior High School Number 50 who will never have heard of Mad-Man Meyers. There will be no pictures to tell your story, Harry. But that is as it should be, after all. Danny is right. Mrs. Wenger's door closes. It is not even difficult to admit, you see: teaching has never given Harry Meyers any real pleasure. I deny nothing by saying so. My brothers did not know so much, after all. I was not so different. I held a job, I married, I saved some money. There is a good chance I will make it past sixty-nine. That is all.

Danny rinses his face in the kitchen sink. I sit up, with my feet on the floor, and I notice how much space there is between my pajama top and my body. "I am going to the bathroom. In the hall," I say. It is easier this way, to announce it. He nods and says he will go when I come

back. We are roommates. I put my bathrobe and slippers
on and as I walk from my room I hear Carlos' voice, rising through the stairwell, cursing his young wife. *"¡Puta!
¡Puta!"* Objects knock against walls. Under me, on the
third floor, Mrs. Wright looks out. She asks me how I am
feeling and then yells in an opposite direction for quiet.
When Carlos' door opens, I move away from the wood
bannister. I close the bathroom door behind me, and sit.
Mrs. Wenger has warmed the seat for me and I am grateful to her. I bring up some phlegm and lean to the left,
spitting it into the sink. Simon and I shared a bed on
Howard Street. Simon, Simon, you knew no shame. You
candled eggs until your death. Well. The earth lies above
all of you now, my brothers. The same is true for your
wives, for aunts, for uncles, for cousins. But it is all right.
As you can see, Harry Meyers has enough visitors. There
must be some nephews and nieces left somewhere, but
they do not matter. You had your arm around my shoulder on the trip, didn't you, Simon? First in the train, and
then in the wagon, we sat next to our father. Down the
left side of my body, from under the armpits, there is some
pain. Nothing is easy anymore. I trace the shapes on the
tiled floor, endless rows of six-sided marble pieces. I wonder if they were laid out in straight rows or if a single tile
was the original center, and all the others were attached
from there, in a widening circle. On Howard Street the
bathroom floor was the same. There is something to be
said for a brownstone. Perhaps I will rescue you after all,
Sarah. I told you about that trip, I remember. We visited
the chicken farms which sent us our eggs. It is the first
time I can remember going beyond New York. I could
not have been more than five years old and Simon and

I wore our good suits. I had never seen such farms before. By comparison, the ones in Brooklyn were gardens. I will tell you something: it was a real adventure to journey over dirt roads and have my father make transactions. Simon and I were allowed to play with the baby chickens. And I think I understood the connection between these distant New Jersey farms and my father's butter and egg warehouse. I was not a simple child, after all. It seems strange now to think that some of those men, dressed like true cowboys, but without beards, were Jews as we were Jews. I must have thought all the Jews in America lived in New York City. You loved my father, Sarah, didn't you, though you knew him less than a year. Well, I am entitled to a few memories. The visiting hours are not yet over. I hear steps. I am interested in what Jackson's brother had to say this time, but I can wait to see the note. Let Danny have some pleasure. I will be better soon. We will evaluate my situation. His original suggestion may be worth considering. Another trip does not sound so terrible to Harry Meyers. The room, as Danny suggests, is not adequate, and I do not fool myself really, about what the pictures will add.

Outside, it is totally silent, and then, suddenly, a high-pitched shriek splits the air. It is followed by the sounds of bodies struggling. I have been finished for some time. I take care of myself, then put my robe back on. I pull the chain but even the rush of water does not drown out the sound. Perhaps the tiles were laid out in diagonal rows, beginning in a corner.

"Aiee — !" A body crashes against my door. It is my fault. I should have said something before. I did not think. "*¡Ahora,* Manuel! *¡Asesino!*" Mrs. Wright is on the landing again. She promises to move from the building tomorrow morning. Carlos no longer needs to curse his wife. He sends his abuse in my direction. Mrs. Wenger's door does not move.

In my room, the action is almost completed. Marty's head is jammed in the opening of the fireplace, against the black metal. His beret lies on the floor next to him. Danny's hand is locked at his throat. Manuel crawls along Danny's striped pajamas, his fingers clawing at his back. My other monkey is dancing and singing, his fist clenched above his head. He asks Marty if it is time to use it, but Marty does not give him the signal. He gags and continues to struggle. Ruben takes the pins from my doll and begins sticking them into Danny's legs. "Now, Manny boy —" Marty says. Manuel opens his mouth as wide as he can, then clamps his monkey's teeth into the back of Danny's neck. Danny howls and as he reaches behind him to get at Manuel, Marty gives him a vicious chop with the side of his hand. My guardian rolls onto his side, away from the fireplace. Ruben dances with delight. *"Ahora,* Manuel," he chants. *"¡Ahora!"* Something shines in Manuel's hand. He yanks at Danny's hair, but the greasy strands slip through his fingers. "The scalp," Marty says. His forearm is pressed across Danny's neck, Manuel's legs surround his stomach, and now my own monkey sits astride his thighs, backwards, working at his feet. I think of Gulliver, tied down by his own monkeys and I wonder if there has ever been a Spanish-Hebrew version of that. Ruben's hands move up and down. Danny is choking. I move forward to separate my visitors. They have not noticed me.

"The scalp," Marty whispers. "The scalp —"

"Enough," I say. "Stop — "

Marty turns toward me. A gurgling sound comes from Danny's throat. He can neither move nor speak. In the middle of the floor, on my rug, he seems to fill the entire room. "Is this joker — ?" Marty stops to catch his breath. "Is he a friend of yours, Meyers?"

"Yes," I say.

"Easy then, Manny boy," Marty says. His breathing is difficult. "Easy." He lifts his forearm. "And don't you try any smart stuff, mister," he says to Danny. "We're taking Meyers' word, you understand?"

Ruben stands and places the pins back in my doll. Danny sits up. He rubs at his neck where Marty has been applying pressure. "Put the blade away," Marty says, his arm around Manuel. He speaks softly. "Some other time — right?"

Manuel retreats to a corner of the room. He squats, and, in the shadows, I see only the red glow of his cigarette.

Danny is in a daze. He holds a handkerchief where Manuel has done his work. "They are boys from my school," I explain to him. "It is all right — "

"Yeah," he says, and turns away from me. He feels he has let me down, I know. He is embarrassed. There is nothing I can do. It would be useless to tell him that it was three against one, for they were only boys.

"I told you, didn't I?" Marty is saying. He is close to me, his beret perched once again on the side of his head. "A born killer. If you hadn't stopped us — "

"I am sorry," I say to Danny. "I should have told you I was expecting them to return. They were here earlier today. They were the ones who brought me the cans of juice."

E

Danny has put his bathrobe on. He opens a can of beer and his hand is trembling. "How much do I owe you kids?" he asks Marty.

"Forget it," Marty says.

"C'mon," Danny says. His voice is stronger. "What's fair is fair — we don't want no charity — "

"Make it two bucks," Marty says, and he winks at Ruben. My monkey's eyes are shining.

"You sure?" Danny says, and, from his pants, which hang over the easy chair, he takes his wallet. Marty says that he is sure and Danny hands him two single dollar bills.

My monkey has discovered something, I see. He moves closer to Danny. Suddenly his eyes open wide and he is smiling. "I know you!" he exclaims. He twists his lopsided head toward Danny. "You the father," he says. *"Mi madre,* I am sorry. Oh man — if I see your face at the beginning we not jump you like that — "

"Jump me?" Danny waves a hand at him. "C'mon, kid, don't tell me no stories — you walked in here and I got you before — "

Ruben ignores Danny's protest and turns to his leader. "He is the father in the pictures!" he says. Marty looks at Danny carefully now, and nods his head. Everything will be all right, I know. Ruben's eyes move downward. "We sorry about your boy," he says.

"Sure," Danny says. He looks at me. He has regained some of his composure. Ruben seems sad. He does not have anything else to say. He too is thinking about the pictures. Manuel sits silently in the corner. Marty is at my desk, waiting. Danny is at my side. "Listen — do they know about —" His voice is low. He hesitates. "You know — the notes — ?"

"No," I say. "There is no need — "

"You mean Jackson's brother?" Marty says. He comes to us. Danny is surprised at first. Marty laughs and pats him on the back. "Take it easy," he says. "We know, right?" Danny leaves me. He is puzzled, but he looks at me in a way which makes me certain that he and Marty understand one another. I knew it would happen, you see. Danny rubs his chin. He seems almost ready to assert himself and, in truth, I am happy for him.

"That's why I come here, see," Danny explains to them. They are quiet. He has their attention. He begins to re-count the tale of what he will do to Jackson's brother if he should visit us. Manuel rises from his corner and listens with the others. They sit in a semicircle around Danny, on the rug, and they look with envy at his suitcase. "If I'd of known you kids were keepin' an eye on Mister Mey-ers I never would of jumped you like I did — "

"It's okay," Marty says, and reaches out with his right hand. Danny takes it and then he shakes the paws of each of my monkeys. They have an alliance, you see. Harry Meyers has nothing to fear any longer. "We got our plans too," Marty says.

"I gotta get rid of this beer belly if I'm gonna be any use, though," Danny says. "I never should of let you guys get me the way you did — "

"It was three against one," Marty says. "And we got tricks — "

"The spots," Ruben whispers. "Show him the spots."

"Once is enough." Marty's voice is sharp. Ruben is quiet.

"But I don't know what Jackson's brother looks like, see, and in the dark, you — "

"It's okay. You were just doing what we would have done, right?" Marty says. "We should've identified ourselves — "

Then Danny explains to them about living with me for a few days, until I am better, and Marty suggests that they share the assignment. He says that if Danny has to go to work in the morning, they can return and take a shift. I sit on the edge of my bed and wonder if I will be able to sleep again. Now that I have lost a day my schedule is off. Well. That is all right also. I can watch over Danny while he sleeps and make certain he does not attack other visitors. Carlos is much bigger than Ruben. I could not assure a happy ending there.

"I bring you the surprise," Ruben says. He is sitting next to me while Marty and Danny make their arrangements.

"Of course," I say. Manuel is in the corner again, smoking. Perhaps I will talk to Mr. Greenfeld. I cannot be responsible, after all. I wonder who else will be visiting today. Morris is late.

From under his shirt my monkey slips something. "I seen you," he says, and puts the glossy papers in my lap. I turn the night-table lamp on, so that my likeness may look also. "This the surprise," Ruben says. In my lap are the pictures from the bulletin board. I laugh. They are not the ones I will request when the year ends, but the others, the ones that tell of the future. "When we finish with our work, we sneak into the school and I get them for you from the wall. It give you something to read while you sick."

"Thank you, Ruben," I say, and not without pleasure, I look at the full-color pictures which are so familiar to me. With Danny only a few feet away I read again about the gift of life from the dead: the man's kidney rushed into the body of Mr. Wolf Sturmer of Cleveland. If he is restless, I will let him read sections also. We should share such things. Ruben smiles. His gift, he sees, has pleased me. Wolf Sturmer's body struggles against the tissue of an alien kidney, and, temporarily victorious, he puffs happily on a cigar. Ceramic hip joints, silicone rubber breasts, blood pressure regulators: Harry Meyers may have need of them, after all. I do not hold it against you, Sarah. How could you know. If I go beyond sixty-nine it will have to be on my own. It is best that way. "Nobody seen us," Ruben says. "We hide in the laboratory when the janitor go by. We have fun going through the building with nobody there." He laughs. "Manuel, he want to hide in Mr. Greenfeld's closet to wait for him in the morning, but we get him out — " A woman's life is prolonged by being tied up to a pig's liver. The pig's snout sticks out from under blue sheets and it amuses Ruben. Silently, Manuel has crept to us. He leans over Ruben's shoulder, entranced by the pictures. He has stopped smoking. Marty and Danny continue their discussions while, with my monkeys, I consider the question put to us: will women be content with prefabricated embryos?

"We be going soon," Ruben says to me. My eyes close momentarily, and this time I see nothing. "We just come by to check." Manuel holds a picture in his lap: a wine-red monkey fetus is being withdrawn from its mother's womb. Gently, the doctor's fingers lift its veined body. Manuel's eyelids rise.

"He thinks that one of the sewer babies," Ruben says to me.

"Of course," I say. Perhaps I will get copies made and

give them to the old men who walk to the synagogue each morning so that they too will be prepared. It is something to consider. Manuel's finger traces the outline of the fetus across the page. The colors are vivid. When I have removed my pictures also, there will be little in the school to interest students. Before I leave I should give my suggestion concerning mirrors to the principal. It would be something.

"In the projects lots of the girls put them down there," Ruben is saying. "Sometimes they not born all the way."

"Of course," I say.

"Manuel, he think if you go crawling around the sewers and tunnels under the city, you gone to find armies of these kids that been growing up there."

"It is a thought," I say. I place the article on my night table. I feel the glands move along my throat. It would be nice if the fireplace had not been sealed over, I think. We could have a good talk now, the five of us. Manuel hands me the page. He goes back to his corner. "What you think?" Ruben asks. "You think it really could happen — ?"

"It is a thought," I say.

Ruben nods. "There enough garbage and small animals there for them to live on, but most of them, when they get born, the women wrap them in newspapers before they drop them down." He is thinking.

"It could happen," Marty says, joining us. "There've been kids brought up by wolves and things."

"Indians," Ruben says, his eyes beginning to glow. "You have told us."

"And once there were a few packs of them roaming around, they could take care of the new ones that got dropped in — but what you have to think about is how they get past that first year or so, when they can't cope for themselves, right?" He stops and looks at me.

"What you think, Mister Meyers?" Ruben asks.

"It is a thought," I say.

"Okay, kids," Danny says, and his hands actually touch the shoulders of my students. "How about taking off now so Mister Meyers can get some rest. We'll see you tomorrow morning, okay?"

"Marty is an expert on the American Indian," I say. I will contribute something also, I have decided. It is not fair merely to take from my visitors, to be only an audience. "He knows a great deal."

Ruben's eyes shine. "That the truth, mister," he says to Danny. "He can walk up high with the steel men and not get scared, like the Indians do in Brooklyn."

"Brooklyn — ?"

"Gowanus," Marty explains. "Where all the Mohawks live. North Gowanus, actually — you're from Brooklyn, right?"

"Yeah, but I never — "

"If you come with us when Meyers here gets well, I'll introduce you to some of them."

"They are beautiful," Ruben says. "Their hair is like coal, their skin is copper."

Marty nudges me with his elbow. "You know what I think is gonna happen?" he says to the others. The room is hushed. "I think the Indians are waiting, just waiting. And they're gonna be here when we're all dead and gone, and then they're gonna go down into the sewers and rescue all the packs of wild kids."

Manuel edges forward. His eyes are on fire. Ruben is

nodding vigorously. "We are part Indian," he says, proudly. "Marty has told us. Indian and Spanish and Negro." He looks at Manuel. "But more Indian than Spanish and more Spanish than Negro — "

"Yeah," Marty says. "Sure, Ruben baby. The Spanish weren't so hot to the Indians either, you know."

"That is why Manuel and I gone to learn to walk high," Ruben continues, and he steps lightly across the room, one foot behind the other in a straight line. "Someday we will own the land again, Mister Meyers. You gone to see. It has been written."

"It is a thought," I say.

"C'mon, c'mon," Marty says. "We gotta settle down for the night and let Meyers here rest up."

"It has been written," Ruben repeats. "You gone to see, Mister Meyers."

"Cool it, Ruben — let him get some shut-eye."

Perhaps, I think, the great Don will return to lead the packs of children. Marty would appreciate the thought, I know. The book is not on my desk. I had intended to give it to Ruben, though I do not recall doing so. I look through the three shelves of my bookcase, next to the desk, but it is not there either. I check my night table. "C'mon, c'mon," Marty says. "Let's split out — " He seems nervous. I ask if anybody has seen a copy of *Don Quixote* in the room, and my monkey exchanges glances with his leader. Manuel slides more deeply into his corner. It seems ridiculous, yet I know at once what has happened. Harry Meyers has not been a teacher all these years for nothing.

"You took the book," I say to Marty. "This morning." He shrugs.

Danny moves toward him, his arm pulled back, his fist clenched. "Hey," he says. "If you kids are stealin' from — "

"Hold your horses, Danny boy," Marty says. "It's only a book." He looks at the floor. His back is to the fireplace. "What do you think — people *own* books? What makes you think it belongs to you, huh? Books are books, Meyers. You're supposed to be the teacher, you should know that, right? So explain to me: how can you *own* a book somebody else wrote, huh?"

Danny is about to grab my young scholar. "It is all right, Danny," I say. "I must have left it at school. It is all right."

"If you need it so bad, we'll get you another copy," Marty says. "I'll give Manny the order, right?" He adjusts his shoulders and picks at his braces with his fingernail. "I'm surprised at you, though, Meyers, thinking that way." He is himself again. His uneasiness is gone. "The Indians, see, most of them didn't think things like books belonged to anybody. The same with land. That's how come they got cheated so much." Ruben moves his head up and down. His education continues, you see. Danny does not seem very certain of things. Well. I will reassure him later. "Private property," Marty says. "Where's it get you in the end is what I want to know — "

"Yeah? Well you just watch yourself," Danny says. "Indians or no Indians. You write your reports for school — I got nothing against that, but you leave your cock-eyed theories behind if you want to be able to come here again."

Marty laughs. "Sure," he says. "I'm with you, Danny boy, don't you know that?" He takes him into his confidence, apart from his two monkeys, and whispers to him

E*

what he has already told me, about keeping his assistants in line. That is the reason for the speech we have just heard. His stories, Danny admits, patting him on the back, have something to them. He predicts that Marty can be a marvelous salesman someday, if he wants. He opens the door. "It has been written," Ruben says again. "You gone to see, Mister Meyers. Someday — "

On my night table I look at my new reading material. There was no real need to complain about the loss of my book. I should have considered more carefully. "Listen," Marty says and once again Harry Meyers is in his confidence. "I want things to be straight between us, you understand?"

"Of course," I say.

"About the book, I mean." I nod. "We're all entitled to our theories, right?"

"Of course," I say.

Ruben is speaking to Manuel of the sewer babies and the great day on which they will all be released into the sunlight. "I mean, we understand one another, right?" His breath is sweet, though I cannot place the fragrance. I realize that I have forgotten once again to look into my monkey's eyes, to see what color they are. He will be back in the morning, though. When I first began teaching at Public School 50 the gypsies lived in storefronts along Broadway. Their scarves were of beautiful silk, brightly colored. They wore no shoes. If you did not watch out they would come in the night and steal your children. Ruben would have loved them, I know. Perhaps Harry Meyers did find some pleasure in his teaching then. But it was not much. "I just didn't want you thinking I was one of these guys on some kind of Give-America-Back-to-the-Indians Crusade. That's a lot of crap, right?"

Ruben is speaking to Manuel of Señora Rosa's prophe-
cies. Danny is becoming impatient. "And don't let any of
the propaganda the National Indian Youth Council puts
out fool you." If visitors continue to come, perhaps I will
stay indoors for a while. At least until the end of winter. The subways, the slush, the ice: there is no need for
such things, after all. I am entitled. "They're young and
nationalistic, sure, but if they've got three thousand members they've got a lot, right?" I wonder what Manuel's
sister looks like. It is something I can ask Ruben tomorrow morning. It is too late now. If they are all here together when I awake, perhaps Danny will ask me to tell
the story again. It would be a way for Harry Meyers to
contribute something. "The way I see it, and here I'm
not just telling stories, they're not gonna have to take it
back, and nobody's gonna give it to them." He licks his
lips. I am grateful to Danny, you see. I only hope he will
be able to sleep well in the easy chair. I will reassure him
again about the book. Marty's voice rises. "Like I said
before, if you don't believe in property and competition,
you don't have much chance to cope in this world, right?
So they're waiting, that's all. Waiting, you hear me — ?"
His hand tugs at my bathrobe sleeve. There is urgency
in his voice. "They'll still be here when the white men
are all under the ground, when — " He seems aware suddenly of his intensity, the passion with which he has been
speaking, and he breaks off. "It's just a theory," he says,
shrugging. "We're all entitled, right?" His green bag is
slung over his shoulder. "And we know all that crap
about confusing our wishes with — you know — " He
moves away from me. "Every joker has to have his way of
coping in this world, right, Meyers?"

"Of course," I say.

He winks at me. "One of these first days," he says, and gives me a brief wave of farewell. Let me tell you something: there will never be enough policemen to guard the hospitals. I am certain of it. The picture of what will happen, though, is too much for me to contemplate now. It is enough if I think about returning to school. I laugh to myself. Harry Meyers cannot even do what he does not want to do. Well. It is something to think about.

"Tomorrow," Danny says, and closes the door behind them. He comes into the room, shaking his head. "Nutty kids, huh — ?"

I nod.

He yawns. "Boy, I'm bushed." He shakes his head again. "Especially that Marty. I mean, don't get me wrong, he means well and all that. But — " He nods affirmatively. His voice changes. "I got to hand it to you, Mister Meyers, the way those kids respect you. All the things they're trying to do for you — it's really something!"

"It is something," I say.

"I guess you got to be real dedicated like Jean always says about being a teacher." He laughs. "That little one is something, though, ain't he? Just keeps puffin' away. You know why?" I indicate that I do not. "It's so he don't get no bigger. Marty told me." He scratches his head. "I didn't think anybody believed that stuff anymore about smoking stunting your growth, but I guess there are some things that never get lost, you know what I mean?" He leans forward. "It's for his job, from what Marty says."

He talks a while longer, and I know it makes him feel better to share his impressions with me. He tells me that I already look one hundred per cent better than I did when he first came by this afternoon. What I need is more sleep.

"When you meet a kid face to face it's hard to hold anything against him, you know what I mean?" he says. His feet are propped on my desk chair, and he is using the bedspread to cover himself. We will get along together, you see. "I mean, you can see that he's just a kid like any other kid — the Puerto Rican one, I mean — "

"Yes," I say.

"It makes you think," Danny says. My eyes are closed. "I bet the Spanish kids you got are like him mostly — different than the colored, I mean." He stops. "If not for the accent, I'll tell you the truth, some of them could pass for wops!" He takes pleasure in this observation. "Ah, I'm really bushed. But it's the truth, Mister Meyers — especially those who come from the south of Italy, you know? They could look like you and me." I watch my guardian. He turns onto his side, but this will not do. He sits up straight, his feet forward, his hands clasped on his chest. He does not wish to keep me up, he says. His voice is gentle. "You get a good night's sleep, Mister Meyers." I pull the chain on my night lamp. The room is dark. I am not at all tired, though. I arrange the pillow behind me and sit up, my back against it, looking ahead. After a while my eyes adjust and I can see my guardian. His mouth is open. He has not even suggested that I recount our story. Our bonds grow deeper.

When he begins to snore I get out of bed. I put on my slippers and cross the room. I lift the side of the window shade with a finger and look down into the street. Through the windowless openings in the front of building number 171, I see light. I have my glasses on. I am certain of it this time. There is a fire burning. Well. We know where the next shift waits, don't we.

In some upper floors of the brownstones across the street, lights are still on. I am more fortunate than most, I realize, to have so many visitors. I hear a rustling sound behind me. Danny does not stir, but a new note, I know, has just been passed under the door. I leave it. I will let Danny discover its contents in the morning. It is the least I can do for him.

I hope my other three are warm. If they had stayed here, I know, Danny would never have slept. I need not worry about them, though. They will manage. Marty will tell them stories. It was winter when we rode across New Jersey. My father's beard was still black. He was not an old man. He hummed and talked to the horses. Simon had been with him on previous trips and he explained everything to me. I remember holding a baby chicken. I could not have been more than five years old. When we returned was the only time in my life I showed any interest in the warehouse, any pride in the sign (*Meyers Butter & Eggs*. They could not get me to help, even in the busy seasons. I do not blame you, Simon, if you do not forgive me. But were we to do it over again, I would not change, I assure you. Perhaps, then, it is time for another trip. Danny snores. My sinuses are still clear from Marty's medicine. If Morris should come by I hope he will not be jealous of my arrangements. It is only temporary, believe me. Danny has his own family to go to.

The windows are frosted, yet the snow and the ice do not bother me. I fear the summer more. I wonder if I can place an order with Manuel for an air-conditioner. Let the note lie on the floor, Harry. After all these years it is silly to be afraid of dreams, and, in truth, I am not. A figure emerges from the entrance to my building and runs toward Amsterdam Avenue, diagonally, across the street. He is very fast. The fire is a small one. I will return Nydia's pot tomorrow. I wonder if the Rebbe will come to visit me. Danny would get along with him also, I think. As for Marty, I make no predictions. We will see, Harry. Think about it. My new roommate may be right. Where we first lived, on the lower east side, there was a shop around the corner which made cigars. The odors were beautiful and the owner hired a little man with a long beard to stand on a table and read stories in Yiddish to the workers as they cut and rolled the leaves. I will have to tell Marty. It is a trade he would have been suited for. The owner would shoo us from the front, but we had our ways also. I heard many stories, I can tell you that.

SIX

I AM READY. I know it as soon as I wake up. Once again my sleep has been dreamless. I am on my side. The room is warm. Danny is already gone and, though I did not hear them enter, my three young guardians have taken up his vigil. I will shave this morning, and dress in my good black suit. I can smell raisin wine. Like our father, Simon used a lime preparation to remove the hair from his face. Razors were forbidden. It must be the same with my cowboys. I remember that fragrance also. It was not unpleasant.

Manuel sleeps in a corner of the room, underneath the window, his head resting against the wall. My own monkey lies where Danny slept last night, the bedspread across the lower half of his body. He too sleeps on his side. Well, I wish you long life also, Ruben Fontanez. But you should begin practicing now. The years go by, you see. His knees are folded toward his chest. In his hands he holds a doll. My other warrior is at the window, surveying the street from behind the window shade.

Under my pajama top I scratch at my chest, and come away with curled hairs pressed between my fingers. You look peaceful now, my monkey, but I am not fooled. Harry Meyers does not forget so quickly. He remembers the dream. He remembers the pins. In the restaurant I was gentle with you. Now, with your mother's death, I will not press you. But soon, my monkey. Soon. Harry Meyers will know.

"Good morning," I say, and my two monkeys stir.

"What's the good word?" Marty asks. He raises the window shades. Ruben rubs his eyes. He is still on his side. Manuel lights a cigarette. "You feeling any better — ?"

"Yes," I say, and sit up. "Yes." The aching in my side has left, and I feel, in truth, as if I have been sleeping for years. My head is clear. I wonder, in fact, if more than one day has passed since Marty and Danny consummated their agreement.

"Good," he says. "I told you, didn't I? Sleep and fruit juices. Then let nature take its course, right?" He ruffles Manuel on his greasy head, then comes closer. "And keeping this room warm. That's important. The Mandans used to have steam baths where they used wild sage — guaranteed to knock a cold out of a man within half a day — " He grinds the knuckles of his right fist into the top of Ruben's skull. "How's it going, Ruben baby?" he asks.

Ruben pushes his hand away. He is not smiling. "I dream of my mother," he says.

"It figures," Marty says, and walks away from him. "You

want me to fix us some chow for breakfast — ?" He opens the refrigerator. "Soft boiled eggs would be the best thing for you. Keep off fried stuff for another day or two, till your system's cleaned out — "

"I dream of my mother," my monkey says again.

"So what do you want us to do — ?" Marty asks. He shakes his head. "Big deal. Listen, Ruben baby, the old lady's dead — kicked the bucket, gone, passed away, kaput, finished, *muerto*, on ice — you understand? You got guilt problems, you peddle them somewhere else, you hear?"

"Her mouth was full of dirt — " He goes on as if he has not heard Marty. His voice is strong. "All my younger brothers and sisters danced around her." He lifts the bedspread from his body and comes toward me, the doll in his hand. "They would not let me into their circle. I stood behind — "

"Listen, I said to cool it, Ruben," Marty says as he carries eggs and milk from the refrigerator to the kitchen table. "If that dirt in your pocket's bothering you, just give it here and I'll find good use for it — "

Ruben tugs at my pajama sleeve. "Her mouth was full of dirt, Mister Meyers." His eyes, I see, are an olive-green shade, tending toward brown at the edges. I am certain they change to shades of gray also. It would depend on the lighting. *"Mi madre,* Mister Meyers. *Mi madre.* What I gone to do?"

The doll in his hand, I see, is not the one of me. That still rests on my night table. This one is larger. The head has been fashioned around a light bulb and under the white and pink paint, I see the vague columns of newsprint. "I am an old man," I say, and pull my sleeve away from him. His eyes are desperate. *"Mi madre,* Mister Meyers. *Mi madre.* What I gone to do?"

Marty is suddenly behind him, and, with the back of his hand he whacks my monkey on the side of his head. "Snap out of it now," he says. "Shake it up, Ruben. You heard what Meyers said — we don't need all this stuff about your old lady's funeral while — "

Ruben whirls around and, with his forearm, he slams his leader across the chest. His eyes are on fire. "You don't tell me what to do about my mother," he says. *"¡Batardo!"* he hisses. Manuel rises and moves toward his friends. I see him touch his side pocket. "I not scared of you, man — " Marty looks at Manuel, then at Ruben.

"Okay, okay," he says, and turns his back to us. "Take it easy. Cool off — " He faces us and smiles. He has decided quickly. "It's okay if you dream about your mother — and I'm sorry if I said anything, right?"

My monkey's hands drop to his sides. The fire leaves his eyes. He breathes quickly and shrugs his shoulders. Marty is at his side at once, his arm around him, his mouth close to my monkey's ear. He walks him to the window, then back to the kitchen, and as he whispers, Ruben nods his head up and down. A dream is only a dream, Ruben Fontanez, I think. But Marty will take care of you. There is no need for Harry Meyers to intercede. He must prepare for other things. Manuel too sees that the crisis is past. He returns to his corner. His eyes look out above the window ledge.

I put my bathrobe on. We could continue to live like this for years, I know. They would take care of me. Danny and Marty would be in charge. Well. If they have been considering such an arrangement, that is their business. It is nothing to me. Ruben is at my side. "You will see, Mister Meyers," he says. "When it is time, we will rescue my brothers and sisters and take them to live with us."

"You like your eggs real soft or a little on the medium side?" Marty asks.

"Medium," I say.

I listen to the sound of pans and silverware. You should not encourage them, Harry. Do not fool yourself. You have been part of the arrangement also. It has not been unpleasant for you. It is all right to keep the earth, my monkey. It is nothing. The Spanish claimed that the Marranos cut out the hearts of Christians. They used them to work the magic which enabled them to escape the Inquisition. You would enjoy the story, but Harry Meyers will not tell it to you. Your envelope will have to be enough, I am afraid.

"I make this doll last night, after you leave. What you think?"

"You have a talent," I say. I look into my monkey's eyes. They are deep-set. His nose is slightly hooked. Who knows, Ruben Fontanez, I think, perhaps somewhere in your past, before the journey across the Atlantic, there were underground Jews in your history also. It would explain things. I look more closely at the doll and see that the nose is quite large. The pins have not yet been placed. There are hairs glued to the pipe cleaner arms.

"I mean, what you really think?"

"I would not show it to him, if I were you," I say. "He might not understand — "

Ruben laughs. "Man," he says. "I not stupid." Marty places a glass of juice in my hand and I drink. It is apricot nectar again and it is very soothing. "You want some jam on your toast?" he asks.

"All right," I say.

"Ruben's right, you know," Marty says, as he returns to his work. "Now I've got nothing against your friend — but in our position we can't afford to take chances, right? That's why Manny's watching the street now." He unscrews the lid of a jar. He is enjoying himself. If his life could be spent planning such things, I think, he would always be happy. "We'll hang around a little while, then we'll have to set up our lookout from somewhere else."

I walk to the table and sit down. Ruben sits across from me. I crack open my egg. "I'm not saying I don't trust him, I'm not saying I do — we just can't take chances, that's all." I sprinkle some salt on my egg and watch Ruben do the same. "We were just waiting for you to get up, see, so we could tell you our plans. You ought to know — "

Ruben smiles. "Tonight," he says, fondling his new doll. "Tonight I take this to the Black Mass." His eyes flash. "We find out the truth — "

"*Bruja*, right, Ruben?" Marty says, and he joins us at the table. He gives me my toast and winks at me. "*Bruja* — "

Ruben nods. "In Harlem," he says. "I will bring the doll and place it on the altar and we will know the truth."

Marty chews his piece of toast. Let me tell you something: if the choice for Harry Meyers were death or baptism, he would choose baptism. "They gonna have a live virgin tonight?" Marty asks him.

Marty is reaching him. "Aiee — " Ruben cries, and

holds the sides of his head. I hear a sound from across the room.

"Keep your eyes on the street," Marty orders. Manuel obeys. Marty turns to me. "He's not telling you stories, Meyers — they hold these things up there, with girls sprawled on the altars and all this voodoo stuff — " He taps with his fork against his cup. "And who are we to say whether it's cock-eyed or not, right? One of these first days we might find out a lot of things aren't as cock-eyed as we thought. And I'll tell you something else." His eyes narrow. I see a spot of egg yolk trapped in his braces. "They get some results. The stuff works. And that's all that counts in this world — "

I smell the tea brewing. The fragrance of raisin wine is lost. When I return, perhaps I will take my cowboys on a field trip. Such a mass would not seem strange to them, I am certain. But you know that already, don't you, Ruben Fontanez. You have looked in their windows. I wonder: I think you would have chosen death, but who can know such things. The great Rebbe Sholem stayed up for one thousand days and one thousand nights reading Torah in order to attain communion with the prophet Elijah. There is such a thing as Satan's Chassidism, you see. I have heard the cowboys argue about it. "You want to come?" The question is from Marty.

"I am an old man," I say, and shrug.

"You not so old," Ruben says. "There's a man — " He looks to his leader, a question in his eyes. Marty considers. Then he gives his consent. "There's a man up in Harlem, he real old. Nobody know how old he is."

"We talked it over last night," Marty says to me. "And we decided to put it to you — if you want to meet him or not — "

"You like him a lot, Mister Meyers," Ruben says. "You never meet anybody like him. Some people say he is one hundred years old — "

"I'm not saying yes, I'm not saying no," Marty says. "If you want to believe it, you believe it." He has his green bag ready.

"You never see anybody so black," Ruben says. I think of Jackson in his powder-blue earmuffs. For one night, at least, I have escaped, but I am certain Danny will request a telling of the story when he returns tonight. "He is our leader, Mister Meyers." His voice drops. "Even Marty let him — "

"Cool it, Ruben," Marty orders. His voice is sharp.

"I am sorry. But it the truth, Mister Meyers — like I tell you once. There lots of kids around the city making it like us, and we all — "

Marty slaps Ruben across the knuckles with the back of his spoon. "You finished eating?" he asks. "This place is beginning to give me the willies. The sooner we split out and take up our lookout, the better I'll like it." He stands and Ruben does the same. "You had another note this morning," he says to me.

I nod. It does not matter. Marty goes on. "Okay, now this friend of yours probably won't go to the cops, but you never can tell, right? We've got to cover ourselves — "

"All right," I say.

"So don't think we're — you know — deserting you or anything — "

"Of course," I say. I wonder, in truth, what it was like during the three days that Jackson and Gil lived in their hotel room together. It is something to consider, I suppose. The medical reports were inconclusive.

"I'll stay on the roof over there and watch the street,"

Marty says. "Ruben, I want you to get up on top of this building, to make sure he doesn't come in through the backyards, and Manny, just to be sure, you'll guard the basement — " I sip my tea. My glands, I can tell, have subsided even more. I touch my neck. Along the right side there is a single friendly gland which insists on staying with me. Under my fingertips it rolls by itself. "We've been too careful for too long to let anything slip now, right? They won't get me, Meyers, you understand? Not now — "

I nod. Marty is slightly puzzled by the expression on my face, but it is not enough to stop him. "Another thing — I almost forgot," he says. "You had a visitor this morning. Some joker with a seeded roll wrapped in a napkin — "

"Morris," I say. "We were boys together — "

"Well, he trailed it out of here pretty quick when he saw us — so who knows who he'll be gabbing to." He smiles from the side of his face. "You should have seen him, though — Ruben called him a cowboy and the guy nearly flipped — "

I turn to my monkey. He looks down. "I sorry, Mister Meyers," he says. "I tell you the truth, I remember what you tell me in the restaurant about him. I just want to have some fun — " I begin to laugh with my guardians. "We try to call him back from the stairs, but he move too fast for us — "

"It is all right," I say. "I will explain to him this weekend in the park."

Marty pats me on the shoulder. "That's what I like to hear, Meyers — "

"In fact," I say, "I will return to school on Monday."

Ruben claps his hands. "See — ?" he says to Marty. "I tell you. Mister Meyers got real spirit. He the only teacher at our school who — "

"Cool it, Ruben," Marty says. He turns to me. "We'll see about that on Monday. You — "

"I said I will return on Monday." I say it calmly. I do not need to ask permission anymore, you see.

"Maybe yes, maybe no," Marty says. "Meanwhile we'll stake out this place and keep an eye on you — "

"When will you go to work?" I ask.

"That's our business," he says. He does not wish to continue the discussion. "Okay, Manny — " he calls. "Let's move out."

"No," I say. "I am sorry, but it is not your business." I am on the offensive now, you see. Marty stands up. I will shave and put on my good black suit. It is decided. "If I am keeping you from going to work — "

"We'll manage, Meyers — you don't worry about us, hear?" He slings his green bag over his shoulder, but his eyes are somewhat uncertain. You cannot intimidate Harry Meyers for long. Marty will have to learn also. "You've got enough of your own stuff to worry about — "

I turn to Ruben. "I would like to meet Manuel's sister," I say to him.

"You like her a lot, Mister Meyers." His eyes glow. "I want to bring her here to meet you, but Marty — "

"Women are a jinx," Marty says. "How many times do I have to tell you that — ?"

"The Indians would not let women be with them when they made their weapons," Ruben says. "Marty has explained to us — "

Marty rolls his eyes. He is impatient. I am sorry, my

young guardian, but this is the way it must be. "Look —
you bring her here, you're asking for trouble, that's all.
You can take it from me." He points and Manuel goes
back to the window. Then he sighs and sits down in the
easy chair. "Okay, Meyers," he says. "Let's keep things
straight between us — what's the gripe? I'll tell you what
— we'll work the night shift, when your friend gets back
to take over, okay? That make you happy?"

From inside my night table I remove my shaving kit. "I
will return to work on Monday," I say, and I smile. "It
is decided."

"Okay, okay — but what's that got to do with us keeping
a lookout for this guy who's after you — ?"

"I think I would like to take a walk," I say.

Marty rubs his chin. "So — ?"

"So there is no need for you to continue — "

"Okay, okay. I got the picture," he says, cutting me off.
I tell him that he does not understand. I am not un-
grateful. I appreciate what he has done for me, but I want
to get out some before I return to teaching on Monday.
My monkey is delighted and he does not try to hide his happiness. Only Danny, I think, would be as happy about
such a change in me. Perhaps I will take Ruben and his
young lady to the restaurant with me one day next week.
We will see. Sarah would be proud. It was what she always wanted, after all. Ruben asks me again about going
to the mass and this time I say that I will consider. I have
other things to do before then, though.

"Here," Marty says. "I forgot," and from his green bag
he takes out a book. I know at once what its title is. I
thank him and put it beside the gift my monkey has
brought me. "We're even," he says. It is a more expensive
edition this time, in Spanish. "And I'll tell you something

else," he adds. "That stuff you and Ruben been reading about freezing people — you don't really put any stock in that hocus-pocus, do you?" Ruben's eyes flicker. It would not be a bad idea if he were to take the pins from my doll and use them for somebody else. "I mean, some of that mechanical heart stuff is okay — I was reading it all before you woke up — but anybody knows you can't freeze internal organs and then thaw them out right." He gets no response from Harry Meyers. "Sure," he says. "Freeze what you want — but nobody's been able to preserve even a mouse for a single day. It all goes cock-eyed in the thawing —"

He will not stop talking now, but it is all right. Harry Meyers is not disturbed by his theories. Nor is my monkey, I see. The cowboys know: all matter contains sparks of God. I take the doll in my hands, from where Ruben has left it on the pillow. I twist the pins and feel no pain. Perhaps you are right. Harry Meyers is not so old. "And don't you think for a minute that we're gonna let you go walking by yourself —" Marty is saying. "Around here, you could be knifed and you'd lay in some ditch over in Central Park for a month before anybody'd stop to see what was the matter —"

I take a clean shirt from the bottom drawer of my dresser. Danny's pajamas, I see, are folded neatly on my desk chair. His suitcase stands between my dresser and my desk. In the frame, Sarah and a younger Harry Meyers appear to be very happy. "You stayed in number 171 last night, didn't you?" I say, and Marty nods his head. He says that all the derelicts and runaways in the city use such buildings. The police do not bother with them, especially in winter.

"There is no need for you to follow me," I say. If visitors come by while I am out, they will have to wait. I am ready to accept Ruben's invitation, you see. It is not fair, I tell them, now that my cold has disappeared, for them to lose another day's work. I will see you in action, my monkey.

"You sure?" Marty asks. He does not like the idea, of course, but it is difficult for him to say so.

"I am sure," I say.

Ruben can hardly restrain himself. "Oh man, Mister Meyers — I been waiting to show you how we work — we really gone to surprise you!"

"Okay, okay," Marty says. "It's your skin, Meyers. But if you land up flat on your back again, don't say I didn't try to talk you out of it — "

I assure him I will not. I must shave now, I say. Marty tells me not to waste time. Now that both Morris and Danny know about them, he says, it is best to hurry from my room. He reminds us about the man from the orphanage who is tracing Ruben's whereabouts, about Mr. Greenfeld, and about the men who search for him. He pauses. I know that he would like me to ask who it is that follows him, but Harry Meyers will not give him the satisfaction. It is not the time for such things. I will do nothing with your vague clues, my young fugitive. Before long, you see, the theories will be stripped away. We will see what we will see.

Marty's reminders have made my two monkeys uneasy. They pace nervously in my tiny room. Through the window I see that the sun is shining brightly over West 76th Street. It did not snow yesterday, despite predictions, so there will be no slush, no ice. There are no great dangers. Mr. Greenfeld will sleep in the lounge. Marty will evade his father and his father's doctors. Ruben has little to fear. He is right, after all. One monkey more or less means little to anyone. They already have his brothers and sisters as hostages. They can play a waiting game.

When I am finished shaving I stop in the hallway. Somebody new has moved into the empty room next to the Oriental. I hear words from a television set. The coughing is that of an old man. I listen at Mrs. Wenger's door. There is no sound. I knock and hear something move inside. That is all. I just wanted to be sure. I return to my own room and step out of my pajamas. When I return tonight I will take a bath. As I change into my good suit, my monkeys do not look at my body. I do not look at it, either. I know it well. My three guardians keep their backs to me, their eyes on the street.

I tie the laces of my shoes, and, after my jacket is on, select a tie. I put my overcoat on. "I am ready," I say. I take the mop. Marty, however, grabs it from me. "Don't be a hero," he says, as we leave the room. "If you get tired, say the word."

On the third floor, Mrs. Wright opens her door to greet us. I smell liquor on her breath. Behind her a plaque in brilliant colors explains why God gave his only begotten son. Still, she has little affection for my three students, I can tell. I explain to her that they are from my official class. On the second floor landing, I knock at Nydia's door, but there is no answer. "She must be in the park with the baby," I say.

"If we're going to work, let's go," Marty says.

"I was not suggesting we visit her," I say.

"Sure," my sullen warrior responds.

I show them the hall closet on the first floor, for the

mop, and I notice that the visiting hours have been taken down from the wall. That is just as well, I think, since Harry Meyers will no longer be receiving visitors. If such a thing happens again I will need larger accommodations. Danny is right. At the very least, a room with another door, to provide for all the entrances and exits. One of the young men who shares the garden apartment opens the door and asks how I am feeling. I introduce him to my three students and he smiles. His apartment smells of cologne.

"I am going for a walk," I say.

He tells me to enjoy myself and I realize that he undoubtedly envies me, to have three such young friends. Ruben cannot stop smiling. I look at him. "I remember," I say to him.

He shrugs. "I no mean nothing, Mister Meyers," he says.

"I remember," I say again. In truth, I am not angry. My hand moves, impulsively, as if to touch his forehead. But I keep it at my side.

There are no messages in my mailbox this morning. Ruben tells me that he did not mean anything. There were things he did not understand. *"Lo siento,* Mister Meyers." Again I tell him that it is all right. He believes me. He talks to me of what Marty has taught him about the Indians, of *heemanehs* and *berdaches,* skilled in embroidery, cooking and weapon-making. "It not so bad to be a fag if you an Indian," he says.

Marty sighs. "Don't mind him, Meyers — you tell him something once, he makes a production out of it." Manuel is at our heels, looking up and down the street. "The coast's clear," Marty says. "This way — " And we walk toward Broadway. It is even warmer today than I had thought it was. In the crevice of my chin there are drops of sweat. At the corner, a crowd congregates outside the Riverside Funeral Chapel. I see the long black limousines lined up at the exit. The cars of the visitors are double-parked along both sides of the street. Sarah looks down on all of us.

Manuel is tugging at Marty's sleeve. He points and I too see the policeman who waits for us at the corner. "Listen, Meyers," Marty says. "It'll be best if you don't stay too close to us — just to be safe. You never know, right?"

"But I promise him!" Ruben objects. "I tell him when he better he gone to see us in action — "

"Just hold your horses," Marty says. He is very tense. "I got it all planned — don't worry." We draw closer to him. "For everybody's sake, it's best if Meyers doesn't associate himself with us. Look: if we want to keep using the building there for a hideout — and if we're gonna be able to stay in the vicinity to keep an eye on Meyers here — there's no point in Johnny the Cop beginning to make any connection between him and us, right?" He lets his words linger in the air. I should not have worn a jacket under my overcoat. "Remember, he's got a reputation in this neighborhood. People know him — and you can bet the city'll be checking with all your teachers from school, right?"

Ruben nods. In the windows of the top floors I see faces of old men and women, looking down. They have several days still until their government money arrives. But the checks are always on time. On that morning of the month they wait downstairs. Next year Harry Meyers will join them. If they read this morning's newspaper they will know who the funeral is for. None of them, I see, stands directly in the middle of the window.

"Okay then," Marty is saying. "If we want to be able to maneuver freely from now on, the four of us, listen to me. The best thing, see, is for you to stay about a half block behind us." He is talking to me, I realize. "We'll keep an eye out so we don't lose you —" At the corner, cars are honking and a second policeman appears and waves them on. A young Puerto Rican boy peddles his Associated Food shopping cart through the traffic. I look behind and see that the garbage-can woman is crossing Columbus Avenue. Morris should try to get her to join his home. I will mention it to him. The doorman of building number 190 holds a car door open for one of his clients. On the other side of the street a couple passes, hand in hand, and I cannot tell which one is the man. They walk gracefully and Ruben's eyes follow them also. We do not look at one another. Danny's doll sticks out of his jacket pocket.

"We'll wait for you in the subway," Marty says. "And you can come in the same cars with us, so long as you don't let on you know us, okay?"

I nod. It has been less than two weeks. I did not realize how much I missed my neighborhood. It will be difficult to move next year. "You gone to be surprised," Ruben says. "Keep your eye on us —"

They move away from me. I wait and then follow. At the corner, most of the people seem glad to see one an-other. They laugh, they chatter, they kiss. The women wear fur coats. "At weddings and funerals," I hear a woman say. Her hair is dyed a bluish shade of gray. From inside the chapel, the widow exits, a handkerchief at her mouth. A young man supports her by one arm. One of the funeral directors is giving instructions to the Negro limousine driver. They are very gentle as they lead the widow to the car. I must wait for her to pass. The sidewalk clears and people sob quietly. Ahead of me, I see that Ruben has backtracked to make certain I know they have turned the corner. Manuel glares at the policeman. Marty may be right about him. I would not doubt it. The widow is in the limousine now. She pleads with her son to allow somebody else to get in beside her, and she looks helplessly out of the car window. "You heard?" a man says to me.

I look into his eyes but I do not know what he is talking about. There is something familiar about his face. "She wants me," he says. "It's terrible, terrible, that it should happen this way — when — " He gestures with his hands, disgusted, and gives me a brief hug. "I'm glad you came," he says. "Believe me — " Then he is in the limousine. He sits in one of the folding leather chairs in the back. He waves to me. I do not move. The limousine edges away from the curb and the crowd is in motion once more. I smell the perfumes of middle-aged women. I move forward through their chattering. My monkey will make dolls of all of you, I think. If he could call Morris a cowboy, there is little he is not capable of. You should not look at Harry Meyers that way! I push forward, using my elbows, and I vow that I will not allow such people to come during visiting hours. Ruben will post the rules. Marty and Manuel will stand guard.

"Don't push so much, mister!" The voice comes from a man who seems almost as small as my smallest monkey.

F

Under his coat, he wears a double-breasted suit. His breath smells like old socks, the smell of the synagogue at the end of Yom Kippur. I do not know how old he is, but it is not my fault if the man who died was younger than he was. "Don't fool with me," I say, and shove him aside. Ruben slips from view. At the corner the crowd is thinner. People bargain with one another for rides home. They should have arranged things before, I think.

Don't you be a fool, Harry Meyers. The voice comes to me directly, so that I stumble. Ahead of me, halfway toward 75th Street, on Amsterdam Avenue, my three boys wait. I am dizzy suddenly and a young helper from the funeral parlor has his eye on me, a jar of smelling salts in his hand. I do not need his aid, do you hear me? But what is this, Harry, I ask myself. A man is dead and you play games with three children. Is this a proper way to finish things — to wander around after two monkeys and a crazy fifteen-year-old? You are in such a hurry to get through the crowd, aren't you, Harry. For what? Dolls, fruit juices, Indians, visiting hours. It is you who are playing the fool, Harry Meyers. Don't you know that? I walk forward anyway, following. The young man sees that I am all right. He looks to the others. But my heart pounds fiercely and my shirt, I know, is already wet from sweat. Don't you play the fool, Harry Meyers. There have been enough games. Enough. The sidewalk rises slightly but I am careful. I slow down and I continue walking in a straight line. A man is dead and you play games with three children. It is insane, Harry.

They are in front of Al's Lock and Key Store now. In truth, they seem quite small. Despite Marty's beret, there is nothing conspicuous about them. They are only boys. I call to them but my lips do not move. Monday I will return to work. Harry Meyers will finish what he starts. He has no choice, after all. I should have stopped the dinners years ago. It will be more difficult now, but they will end. For now, though, I will follow my three students. It is pointless to try to get out of it after I have asserted myself. Marty would know how to manipulate such a change. You can be certain of that. This then, I suppose, is what has been decided, and your doll was not the cause, Ruben Fontanez. You can be certain of that also. My name is Harry Meyers, you see, and I have been teaching at John D. Wells Junior High School in Williamsburg since 1926 and at the end of the year, a month before I am sixty-five, I will be retired. And I will leave the pictures in the glass case. All right?

I follow them past the back wall of the Beacon Theater, past the Dori Donut Shop, the telephone company. The old men and women line the benches around Verdi Square, pigeons at their feet. Beyond them I see the sign for the Rutgers Church, the Hotel Westover. The corner of 72nd Street, where Broadway and Amsterdam Avenue crisscross, is filled with people. If I know Morris, he is sitting in Horn and Hardart's right now, trying to kid with the women who sit in the front section, the one that is roped off for those without escorts. My three children enter the subway kiosk and I follow them across the street. They wait for me on the downtown side of the turnstile. I give the man a dollar and he gives me five subway tokens. I will need some for next week.

The writing on the subway pillars does not interest me. I do not look at the people who wait on the platform. I do not look in the mirrors of the gum machines. I follow my orders and stay at a distance. My three young men confer at the front end of the platform, where it narrows like the bow of a ship. An express train leaves from the uptown side. I look down and watch a thin stream of water flow through the grime and filth between the subway tracks. The steel rails are smooth and silver. Manuel shuffles his feet nervously. In the subways he cannot smoke. I think of his sewer babies and wonder about Ruben's question: if they grow up by themselves, will they know how to speak. I see the lights of the Broadway Local as it enters the station at the far end and sways powerfully toward us. Ruben points. I step back. In the first car, the Negro train conductor appears to be asleep. Sewer babies, dinners, translations, frozen bodies: don't you play the fool, Harry Meyers. Enough. Finish what you have started. You have no choice, after all. But do not play the fool.

The fluorescent lights in the subway car seem too bright. The car is no more than half full. The rush hour is past. That is something I do not look forward to. In the spring, the smell of bodies is something terrible. It is worse when I return from my cowboys than when I go in the morning. Then I can still smell the fragrances of secretaries' perfumes. The doors close and we rumble away through the dark tunnel. Marty enters my car and he holds his drums under his arm. He looks my way but acts as if I am a stranger. My two monkeys pass through the opening between the first and second car, and Ruben slides the door closed behind them. Manuel sits in the corner. Above him is an advertisement of a blond woman with a large open mouth. I think of getting off at 66th Street and walking back home, but that would be pointless, I know. I wonder where Manuel's sister is. Despite the fact that I will no longer have to ride the subways, I do not look forward to the summer. When my windows are open at night the noises keep me awake. Across the street, under the rooms of the old people, the chattering from the Puerto Rican families is endless. I will never sleep on my back. That is certain. Harry Meyers does not fool himself about such things. I remember the sound of beer bottles breaking on the pavement, of radios playing Latin American music. They are louder in hot weather. Perhaps I will move before then.

At 66th Street I close my eyes. I trust Marty to tell me when it is time to get off. The sound of the train knocking through the tunnels is comforting. I have always slept well in subways. There is a high-pitched screeching as we curve toward 59th Street, but it does not bother me. I am feeling much better. The sweat on my back is drying. I touch my throat and cheeks, pleased by their smoothness. Tonight I will convince Danny that there is no further need for him to stay with me. I touch the side of my throat and at first I cannot find the friendly gland. I place it. I am reassured.

The train stops but I do not open my eyes. I hear people shuffle in and out. Next to me I feel somebody's arm, but there is enough room. I am not pressed. Don't you be a fool, Harry Meyers. It is the voice again, though this time, I think, I am merely remembering the sound. I do not stumble or grow dizzy. I do not even sway. It is all right, though, all this talk of whether I will sleep on my back or my side, of cowboys, of monkeys, of Manuel's sister, of glands. It means nothing. I know now, you see. I have told you. I am Harry Meyers and I have been teaching at John D. Wells Junior High School since 1926 and at the end of this year, a month before I am sixty-five, I will retire. I know that my three guardians are at the other end of the car and that I am following them. In truth, it is less complicated this way. Let things run their course. A few silly thoughts can remain. We do not need to dismiss them all at once. It would not be natural for Harry Meyers to deny what he cares about, after all. It is true that he plays games with children, but it is also true that he cares about them. He would not deny it.

It is a thought I can live with. Marty is right about my room giving one the willies. There is no need any longer to accumulate money. I have put away more than enough to defend myself from clinics and welfare. A new room, an air-conditioner, a trip, some mild adventure — if these too are games, that will be all right. Well. It will not be easy to separate from them. I feel drowsy. I will sleep well again tonight. Perhaps, when I have returned to school, I can tell them that the police know something. They have seen us together, I will say. They are interviewing me. We will separate as friends. I wish them well.

And there will be no more dinners. I will think of something there also. Marty is right. One must cope. The tunnel grows longer, pinching together at the end. Specks of light flicker as they move toward the bottom. I see the widow being supported by the young man. A man is dead and you follow three crazy children. I hear more noise.

I open my eyes and see the waists of people all around me. I look over my shoulder and see the sign: Times Square. I do not recall stopping at 50th Street. I cannot see to the front end of the car. Perhaps we have already

been separated. I do not look at the words on the newspaper that the man standing in front of me holds. Near
me, somebody is carrying his lunch. I smell tuna fish. My
eyes close again. It is just as well. There is no need to
check the *Times*. Whoever it was, let him rest in peace. It
is nothing to me. The doors to the train remain open. I
hear the air release itself from the brakes. We idle. It
is warmer now. There are more important things to be
done. I must telephone the Yeshiva before sundown and
explain to them. If I lose the job, though, that will not
be a catastrophe either. I have enough money. The doors
close. We are moving again. I feel myself relaxing.
Things are very black. A pleasant drumming sound rolls
through the car. I wonder if we will ride all the way into
Brooklyn. Perhaps we will visit Marty's Mohawk friends
in Gowanus. It is no small thing to build a bridge. Simon
and I walked over the Brooklyn Bridge together, I remember. Sarah and I did not, though we talked of doing
it. The Japanese Gardens were sufficient for us, I suppose. Who is Sarah, Harry.

I try, but it is difficult to remember anything that happened to me before I was five years old. The trip to the
chicken farms in New Jersey — I cannot, it seems, remember anything on the other side of it. If Marty introduces
me to his friends, I wonder what I will say to them. Someone steps on the toe of my right foot. I open my eyes.
People are pushing backwards and there is a clear aisle
down the center of the subway car. I hear somebody singing in Spanish. There is drumming. Manuel comes
shooting down the open aisle, his feet moving with incredible speed, his arms waving, his face contorted in its
own ecstasy.

My own faithful monkey shakes his hips behind Manuel. To the left, Marty crouches over his drums, his hands tapping wildly. Nobody reads. All eyes are on them. Manuel spins. In his right hand Ruben is holding Marty's beret. He shakes the coins in it so that they jingle like a tambourine. He charms his audience with Spanish lyrics, a tale of the most famous dancer of San Juan. I do not believe the intricate rhythms that pound from Marty's lap. Manuel flies in front of me, Ruben bends down, my pygmy monkey somersaults across his back. He leaps through the air, cartwheeling, flipping his narrow body, making wet sounds from his mouth. Ruben jingles the coins in Marty's beret. All around me people reach into their pockets. Marty rolls his head from side to side, making clicking sounds with his mouth, grunting to his beat. I can see the Rebbe hopping around on one foot. The music is joyous. Who will go disguised from country to country as Ruben Fontanez, I wonder. People are smiling. "Aiee — !" Ruben shouts and Marty rattles his fingertips against his two drums with increasing speed. One hardly hears the subway. Things seem silent. Manuel dances with abandon, then streaks down the middle, and, as the drum roll stops, he flips over in midair, without touching anything. He lands on his toes, then collapses, his thighs split against the dirty floor.

There is some applause. Ruben jingles his cap and goes quickly from person to person. He winks at me. His eyes are deliriously happy. They are gray now. I was right, you see. It depends on the lighting. The train is slowing down. We move into Pennsylvania Station. Ruben is gone. People have resumed their former positions. Entrances and exits are made. We continue to 14th Street.

I look at Marty, who wipes sweat from his forehead, and I recall what Ruben said to me in the restaurant about listening under the windows of the Yeshiva. Let me tell you something: I have seen dancing teams before. One does not ride the New York subways five days a week for forty years and see nothing. But they are the best. None of the Negro groups from Harlem, none of the Puerto Rican teams, not even the gypsies — none can compare with my own subway three. You can believe me when I tell you.

Ruben gives the money to his leader. They talk, then make their way through the crowd, toward the third subway car. An elderly woman in a Persian lamb coat pats Manuel on the head and puts something silver in his palm. Marty's face is fierce with pride. I do not blame him. You would be also. I hum to myself. Then I hear the drumming. I see the people who hold the straps above me lean toward the third subway car. Ruben's voice mingles with the iron sound of the train. I catch only phrases. *"Amarle fué jugar con candela . . . salvo por un pelo . . ."*

When we reach 14th Street, I rise from my seat and follow my workingmen. In the third car Ruben is still making his rounds. Business is good, I see. I go ahead of my students and find a seat in the fourth car. The doors close. The crowds have diminished. Only a few people are standing. Marty sits on the floor this time, his back against the doors at the center of the car. *"¡Mira!"* Ruben cries to his audience. *"¡Mira!"* Marty taps on one of his drums with both hands, then on the other. The beat is slow at first. Manuel's body is elastic. His eyelids droop. He snaps his fingers. The tempo increases. Ruben jingles his coins and I must stop myself from clapping. My body sways. I close my eyes briefly and see my father on the couch. His eyes are closed also. My eyes open and Manuel is turning upside down before me, his hands spinning him from the floor of the moving train. "Aiee — !" Ruben screams and Manuel takes his place at the end of the car. He streaks toward the middle. His body seems feather light as he twirls upside down. I hear the gasp of breath this time. Then Ruben is collecting. *"Gracias, señora . . . gracias . . . Mucho gracias . . ."*

Your charm is undeniable, Ruben Fontanez. The Rebbe would appreciate a visit, I am certain. If you want to invite him to the Black Mass, that would be all right also. Marty walks alongside Manuel, his arm across his monkey's wiry shoulders. I think of the verse written above the prayer room of my cowboys: *All my bones shall praise the Lord.* Perhaps I will meet Marty's Mohawks also. I reach inside my overcoat, inside my jacket, into my back pants pocket. I wipe my forehead with a handkerchief and leave a line of soot on it. We are moving again. Those who have paid for the show look into the next car. Those who did not make donations are bound by their guilt to keep their eyes fixed in their own car. While the train moves I step between the cars. I grasp a handrail. Orange and green signal lights flash by. Below, I know, is water, blackness, wooden ties, silver rails, refuse.

Perhaps it is my subway three who will descend into the sewers and lead the children forth, singing and dancing. It is a story Marty can tell forever. The variations are endless. We are at Park Place. Diagonally across from me, in the far corner, my subway three take a break. It is all right. They are entitled also. At Wall Street I rise and follow them into the sixth car. The train descends

into a tunnel and as my monkeys dance and sing, I know,
the Hudson River flows above us. Ruben has stopped at
the far end of the car and his singing is directed to a beautiful young girl. Her eyes, though, are on me. My heart
quickens. Her hair cuts the sides of her face in straight
lines. It is coal black and hangs past her shoulders. Her
eyes slant slightly. Her cheeks have a high flush to them.
Her skin is earthy. She can be no more than thirteen or
fourteen years old. I am certain of it. Her mouth is full
and sensuous, without paint, and under her thin coat she
wears a gypsy's blouse that reveals the full length of her
throat, the spread of her shoulders. Ruben sings of a
soldier killed in battle, a young wife crying at home. In
her lap the girl rolls a strand of orange beads between
her slender fingers. Her mouth opens and I cannot catch
my breath. I cough, but I do not take my eyes away. She
smiles at me and her lips are gentle. I see her tongue. I
remember Mary Santini and I feel your warmth also,
Sarah. Ruben is gone. Manuel tap-dances from side to side.
The pounding of Marty's bongos echoes that in my own
chest. The jingling of coins is frantic. She brushes her
hair back with her hand. I think she is laughing at me.
Her eyes are soft. Does she know? Ruben is to my left
now and his gray eyes tell me that he sees what is happening. Perhaps this will be your next present for your
teacher, Ruben Fontanez. Together, we will violate
Marty's rules. Manuel heads for the center of the subway
car, but she does not look at him. I hear people gasp. Our
eyes remain on one another. My monkey has told you
about me already. I am certain of it. You would do what
he says. I rub my fingertips against my palms. There is
moisture there, and inside me I feel an aching which

reaches to the bones. I will tell you of the dream, Ruben
Fontanez. Then you will be certain. Listen to me, Ruben
Fontanez. You have not even reached your full height yet.
We slow down and the curved mosaics outside the windows tell us that we are at Clark Street, Brooklyn Heights.
The river is not above us anymore. You know, don't you.
Your young lady will feel her body grow, her shape
change. Things will be more definite. When the train
stops, I close my eyes. They will tell me if it is time to get
off. If Marty were not your leader I think you would do
it. I assure you I would not require much. Merely the
touch. I see you smiling, Ruben Fontanez. The pins do
not matter. I believe what you said. You would do it to
warm an old man's bed. "You not so old, Mister Meyers."
Ah, Ruben, Ruben, it is all right. I do not open my eyes
to listen to you. Your eyes are almost green now. You
have your own dreams. I will rest quietly in my room, I
assure you. You will leave us alone. It is all right with me
if you watch over us. Does she know. I feel a drop of
sweat slide under my left arm. I cannot open my coat.
I dig my nails into the plastic cushion under me. Merely
the touch, Ruben. That is all. The music begins again.
A dream is only a dream, Harry. Don't you be the fool.

She is gone, of course. My three students have returned
to the car we came from. They work in the other direction now. There is no need to ask you about it, my wild-
eyed monkey. Harry, Harry, let things run their course.
Finish what you have started. It is too late for anything
new. Forget what you crave, no matter what Ruben says.
The aching cannot come often. Do not deny that you care,
only stop the games. Leave the pictures in the case. Tell
Danny what you have to tell him. Who is Sarah, Harry.

The performances continue. Above the windows there
is an advertisement that you should read, my subway
three. They had you in mind, I am sure.

EMPLOYERS!
HIRE BEGINNERS
Eager to *earn* and to *learn*
YOU CAN TRAIN THEM *YOUR* WAY!

Well. We know what your reaction would be, don't we,
Ruben Fontanez. I can hear you. I wonder what per-
centage Marty gives you, and who represents Manuel. But
I will make no trouble. It is too late to start anything
new. I am certain you will do all right. It is good that
I have come out of my room for the day, I know, but I am
not so certain the subway ride has been a good thing. We
move from car to car and business continues to be good.
I am feeling weary again, though. It is to be expected.
Manuel is tireless. It will be best, after all, if Marty's
rules remain in effect. They signal to me at Franklin Avenue and I follow them up and over the stairs to wait for
the Lexington Avenue Uptown Express. We are not far
from the Brooklyn Museum now. Manuel, if you will
dance up the sides with the cowboys, I would assure you a
good audience. After Borough Hall, the train is virtually
deserted. My two monkeys sit across from me. Their
leader has decided it is safe and he comes and sits by my
side.

He looks straight ahead and his lips barely move. He
tells me that this is the best morning they have had in
weeks. Their luck has been excellent. Not a single policeman has boarded the trains we have worked in.

"With things the way they are we really have to be careful now," he says. "I mean, some of the cops just look the other way when they see guys like us trying to make a buck — but some are real mean bastards and we have to spend half our time just trying to shake them, you know what I mean?"

"Yes," I say.

"It'll be best if you don't talk to me," he says. "I just wanted to let you know that we're gonna be getting off soon to take a lunch break. If you're feeling bushed and want to get back home, I wanted you to know that's okay with us." Under cover of his jacket, Manuel is puffing on a cigarette. He blows the smoke into an empty cigarette pack. "That Manny, he's really something — he's afraid if he gets too big so people don't think he's a cute little kid — you know, the way all these women smile at him — he thinks some other little spic's gonna take away his job." He looks in my face for a response. I give none. "I don't say yes, I don't say no. I'll tell you the truth, though, Meyers — not many people would reach into their pockets if they knew they'd been seeing a fifteen-year-old putting on our act. They don't mind if me and Ruben look older, but — " The rest of his words are lost in the rush of the train. We have already passed the Bowling Green station, so I suppose I will not meet your Brooklyn friends today, Marty. Let me tell you something else: I am sorry you have explained to me why it is that Manuel smokes so furiously. I look at him now, releasing the smoke into the empty cigarette pack, and I am uncomfortable and sad. There is no need to tell you this. I am thrown forward slightly by the rocking of the train, but I do not lose my balance. I remain seated, a few inches forward, my hands braced against the seat. I hear you again, telling me that Manuel would do anything for you. He is a loyal friend. All right. I believe you. Still, I am uncomfortable knowing.

It is all right if you cannot remember anything beyond five years old, Harry, don't you see? Not everything needs to be revealed. There is hardly time, after all. A Negro man appears at the end of the subway car, tapping a cane against the floor. His sign asks us to help him buy a seeing-eye dog. Marty reaches into his pocket, and, as the man passes us, puts some coins into his cup. His eye sockets, I see, are scarred.

"We're in the same business, the way I look at it — " Marty says. An elderly couple to our left is encouraged by Marty's action. The man nods his head up and down, mumbling his gratitude. "Anyway, this guy's really blind — he does all right this way. Better off without the dog — " Then he explains how to tell the difference between the fake and the genuine blind men in subways, but I am not interested in his theories. And I am not interested in why you are running away, my cunning friend. "I did a lot for Manny," he tells me. "I could tell you stories about the things he had to do to make money before I came along, right?" He is angry for some reason. "So if you want to help out, Meyers, the thing for you to do is to tell your boy Ruben to cool it, you know what I mean?" I do not nod. I do not, in fact, know what he is talking about. We have passed Broadway and Fulton Streets. There are more people in the car. Businessmen with fresh haircuts read their papers and reports. They stay away from my two monkeys. Manuel has stopped smoking. Perhaps, once again, I have missed something.

But that is all right also. "I mean, the way I see it, the world's got kids like them by the bazoojies, right? — and it's up to somebody to make sure they get what's coming to them — " The man to my right reads the *New York Times* editorial page, but I do not try to make out sentences. I see the photographs of the famous men who have passed away within the last twenty-four hours. Marty's drums stay in his green bag. We are at the Brooklyn Bridge–Worth Street station and Marty has stopped talking to me. He clicks his tongue and Ruben and Manuel rise. We exit from the train and walk alongside the green iron gate. Marty recommends that I stay behind them. "When we get outside, though. Nobody can tell here. It's okay."

Ruben and Manuel flank me on the left. "What you think, Mister Meyers?" Ruben asks. Manuel is almost a full head shorter than Ruben. They push through the turnstile ahead of me. Marty nudges me with his elbow. He tells me that before I awoke this morning, he and Ruben had been debating one of the proposals in the magazine articles. They were wondering about my opinion. In those states which permit capital punishment, the condemned man would be offered a choice: death or permanent anesthesia. A skilled medical team would use the man's brain and body for experimental studies. I have read the article, of course. I have considered the proposal. I think I know your feelings, my monkey, dolls or no dolls. You would want to be finished with things also, wouldn't you. And your leader wants only to solidify his control over you now. I sense it. Still, I should answer the question. I look at Marty. It is a strange peace you attempt, my young drummer. I think you would be glad at this point to allow Ruben such a slight victory. You would like me to confirm his fears. You must maintain morale in your organization. All does not go well between you. Before, in the subway car, you were trying to tell me something. Well. It is nothing to me. Harry Meyers does not need extra years.

"So they tinker with my brain," Marty is saying. "Let them have a good time. What's it to me — ?"

"Tell him, Mister Meyers!" Ruben is pleading with me. Manuel lights a cigarette. In this instance, I think, Harry Meyers would choose death. But you should not think it is because he has been intimidated, my friend.

"And who knows what might happen in the future, right? One of these first days they might . . ."

My ears are closed to him. "Tell him, Mister Meyers — !" Manuel blows the smoke into the air. In the change booth a gray-haired woman arranges copper tokens in stacks. "Tell him — " I see a policeman appear from the other side of the booth. He has spotted the smoke. I let myself fall a step behind. Ruben is too upset to notice. Marty is fixing his beret. Only Manuel senses something. He looks at me from under his heavy lids.

"Hey kid — "

They are gone, in three directions. Their speed is amazing. Ruben streaks up the left staircase, Marty the right. And faithful Manuel is bravest of all. He runs directly past the policeman, his cigarette clutched between his fingertips, his narrow body evading the policeman's grasp. It would, in fact, be difficult to hold such a boy. As for Harry Meyers, he is busy purchasing five additional tokens. The policeman starts after Manuel, but he is already out of sight. The man turns to the original exit and shrugs. I stare at him. His jaw is unsteady. He would like to do something that would not leave him appearing foolish, but Harry Meyers will not help him, I can assure you. He stands in the middle of the arcade, his action thwarted. Another train is approaching. The policeman moves now, and leans against the wall, muttering to himself. His words are louder for my benefit: epithets about Puerto Rican children. I show no response. He does not think of making a connection between Harry Meyers and the subway three. We are safe, I know. He slaps his nightstick into the palm of his hand to demonstrate his authority.

I deposit a token and push back through the turnstile. I am done following. I would not trade jobs with you, my friend. If I were to spend my life underground I should prefer not to work alone. When we first met, Marty said something about a position in his organization. I laugh to myself. I do not hold anything against him. He has his reasons, I am certain. Everybody is entitled to a theory. I go down the passageway leading to the uptown express. I glance behind, but the steps are those of a delivery boy carrying parcels on his shoulder.

It is a good thing he did not associate us with each other. Marty, you were careless. But Harry, in truth, you were most careless. Things are nearly done and you take foolish chances. Who knows what stories would be printed if all were known, if their presence in your room were reported in the newspapers. As for sheltering Ruben, it is difficult to know how your monkeys and cowboys would respond to such news. One thing is certain, though: you would no longer be Mad-Man Meyers. And it is best, with less than half a year remaining, to work from habit, to continue with the weapons you are familiar with.

I board the subway car and do not pay attention to those around me. Our train travels across the center set of rails. Beyond them, through the openings between moldy girders, I see the signs for the local stops: Canal, Bleeker, Spring, Astor Place. Above me a set of lights has gone out. Between cars a Negro boy in a red baseball cap surveys us all. A transit policeman pushes him aside, roughly, and swaggers through our car. It would be quite easy, as he passed, for a passenger to slip his gun from his holster. Manuel, I am certain, has considered the possibility.

At 14th Street I wander the corridors and make my way down a long ramp to the crosstown line. My shoes pinch my feet. I have not worn them for almost two weeks. Things seem lifeless here without you, my subway three. I am sorry I did not have time to tell you how exciting your performance was. Tonight will be too late. It too would only prolong matters. It will be difficult to disappoint you, Ruben Fontanez. You will know anyway, though. Soon. Your bones spread every day. You cannot do this forever. Perhaps this summer, you also, Manuel, will find that even the cigarettes cannot stop nature from taking your trade away from you. Marty can advise you then, if you are still working together. I would not count on it, though. My instincts tell me something there also.

The crosstown subway is old and I am more comfortable in it. Red plastic cushions do not interest me much. I prefer varnished straw. I see the boy in the red baseball cap riding in the adjacent car. His face is very black. He stands, but not in the doorway. He learns things also. I should have left my room earlier. There was no need to stay that long. I must, I suppose, have wanted certain things.

I choose to get out at Sixth Avenue. I will change at 59th Street and exit by Central Park. There is no need to pass by Verdi Square again. It is all right to help Nydia. If things are explained properly, Carlos will understand. In the D train I close my eyes. My throat feels strained. Perhaps I should visit the doctor, as Marty suggested. It is still winter and my resistance is not all it should be. I should get ready. Soon I will resume my odyssey. I will travel back and forth again, locked in subway cars with other people's breath, enclosed in classrooms with my students' assorted germs. I will climb the stairs, and push through the supermarkets, and who can predict what my dreams will be like. I will tell you this, though: I would not mind seeing Manuel perform again. There is grace in his body, and I would have to agree with the others that there may be more ways than one to measure a C.R.M.D. I will avoid you, Mr. Greenfeld. It will be best that way. I am not sure I would be able to restrain myself. When the frustrations mount, I will have my monkeys to work on, of course, but there will be little pleasure in that. If my three guardians want to maintain their present hideout, there is nothing I can do about it. And there is nothing I can do about your sandblasted cheek, don't you see? I do not fool myself. When I have decided more definitely, and my move is completed, I can let Danny know, I suppose. In a year, perhaps. When I am settled again. It would not do any harm. He does not have so much in this life.

I change for the AA train at 59th Street, and travel two

more stops, to 81st Street. I get out at the front end and walk up the stairs. I look across the street at the stone wall which surrounds Central Park. I am too tired to take a walk now. At this point, until you reach the Great Lawn, it is uphill. In the playground I see the children climbing in the monkey bars and swinging in the swings. The mothers rest on the benches. I do not buy a paper from the man at the newspaper stand, nor do I take the shortcut by the planetarium, through Theodore Roosevelt Park. Columbus Avenue would depress me. I will need my strength. I proceed along Central Park West. Long lines of schoolchildren wait outside the museum with their teachers. Above them Theodore Roosevelt is flanked by an American Indian and an African. Why should I look at the children. I continue. I can see Ruben leading a charge into the giant war canoe in the lobby of the museum. Still, I do not look at the children. I sense, though, that their faces are different shades of brown, their bodies restless. What can it all mean to them, I wonder.

At the corner of West 77th Street I look up at the turrets of the museum, where the huge eagles watch over us all. The sun is not as strong as it was earlier and the building has a pinkish cast to it. It makes me think that it has been raining. The streets are dry. I pass the New York Historical Society. There are no lines of children here.

The fronts of the brownstones and graystones do not interest me today. There are few trees on West 76th Street. I do not want to meet Morris. I do not look for the garbage-can woman. I would rather not encounter anybody. The top sections of the old tenement windows at Columbus Avenue are made of beautiful stained glass.

A sign in front of Sam's Hardware announces a sale. By this time, I am certain, my subway three have resumed their work. It is colder. There are no limousines parked at the far corner and that is just as well also.

In my room, the radiator has just gone on. I listen to its clanking. Danny's suitcase reminds me of what is to come. It was good of Marty to replace the book. We are all entitled to our theories, after all. Who can say what any man would do were he born with such spots. All right. *Morado,* Ruben Fontanez. *Morado.* I do not look at the magazine article, but I do not move it from my night table. My doll smiles at me. The pins mean nothing. I hang my coat in the closet and take off my jacket. In another day, perhaps, I will take a hot bath. Now I should avoid chills. I will undress in a minute.

I pull down one shade, then move to the other window. An ambulance is waiting in front of the Park West Hospital, double-parked. A man with a white beard moves under me to the synagogue. Across the street, leaning against the hood of an old yellow Buick, looking in my direction, I see the boy in the red baseball cap. He looks straight at me and he smiles slowly from his black face. What is left of the sunlight flashes from a gold front tooth.

SEVEN

DESPITE WHAT WAITS for me in the street below, my sleep has been long and deep. I do not remember dreaming. Let me tell you something, though: I would not mind dreaming about you, Manuel. I stretch my body and find that it does not ache. I curl my feet against the warm sheet and hear the bones in my large toes crack at the joints. Perhaps, together, we will lead a parade down West 76th Street. The children from the sewers and Ruben's brothers and sisters and the old people from Morris's home — they will all come dancing behind us. It would not be an unpleasant dream to have. All my monkeys will have their transistor radios turned up high, my cowboys will be dressed in elegant black silk, my Spanish girls will jangle tambourines above their heads and shake their young bodies to the music. We will march across the city. Who would be able to stop us, after all.

But today, I hear, my guardians have a different journey planned for me. Well. It will be easier to let them have their way. They whisper to keep from waking me. It is all right. As I have told you, Harry Meyers is ready for anything. It is only to Harlem, they say. It is all right. Afterwards, I think, I can tell them that they were right about Danny and the police. You were right, Marty, I will say. He could not be trusted. That is why we must separate, you see. There is no point any longer in thoughts of invading the hospitals. Admit it, Harry. Let them go. I will tell you something: though I see myself behind Manuel, with Ruben and Marty at my sides, marching across the city, and though I know I smile at such a thought, do you think I am unaware of how foolish it all is. I remember stumbling. I do not need to hear that voice again. I know. I have told you already that I am Harry Meyers and that I have been teaching since 1926 and that I will be retired at the end of this year. There is no need to glory in the knowledge. Remember this: the mother of Ruben Fontanez is dead also, and though he plays with the earth from her grave and makes dolls, the fact is not diminished. Though a man may be dead and Harry Meyers may play games with three children, Ruben Fontanez did not come here for nothing. Believe me.

As soon as he hears me stir, he is beside me. The urgency in his voice makes me realize that I will not be able to replace his loyalty so easily. "You don't got to go if you don't want to," he says.

"He can make up his own mind," Marty says.

I feel my monkey's body, pressing against me. "Listen: I *got* to go," he says. Marty has turned on the lamp by the easy chair. Manuel is beside him. "You don't, Mister

Meyers. I telling you something," he says. "You got to listen to me — "

"It is all right, Ruben," I say, and lift my legs from under the covers.

"If you don't want to come with us," Marty says, "all you have to do is say the word and we'll take off by ourselves. It's nothing to me one way or the other."

I know, of course, that if I do not go this time, it will have to be some other time. We should not prolong things. "I will go with you," I say.

Ruben's fingers press into my arm. "He's *loco*, Mister Meyers — I telling you!" His eyes are frantic. "What he did to Manuel — ! He *loco*, Mister Meyers — "

Manuel hisses but Marty keeps him from moving toward Ruben. Well. I was right about that also, you see. My instincts have not deserted me. Ruben stands in front of me, ready for his two comrades. Marty was right about Manuel, though. I can see it now. His body is poised. Despite his superior size, my own faithful monkey would not stand a chance. "Easy, Manny boy," Marty says. "Easy. You just stay put now." He walks toward Ruben and I see my monkey's fingers curl into his palms. "You too, Ruben baby," Marty says, but he senses that Ruben is not going to let him by. He considers, momentarily, and he chooses to stop. He sits down in the chair by the fireplace and avoids looking at my monkey. "Okay, Meyers — I'll give it to you straight, otherwise Ruben here won't rest easy," he says. "And we all have to work together on this, right?" He makes a sucking sound as he slides the inside of his lower lip across his top row of teeth. Ruben does not move. Manuel crouches, puffing on a cigarette. His right hand touches his pocket. What I see

now is no dream. Like my own monkey, I can sense what
the end would be and I am not embarrassed by such fears.
It would not be so bad, after all, if Danny would, in fact,
do what I will say he did. Marty is very calm now and this,
I realize, disturbs me more than anything else. I would
rather be going. We should be done with things. I reach
for my shoes. "All that happened was this, see — "

"He try to *kill* him, Mister Meyers — ."

Manuel springs from the floor, but Marty gets to him
quickly and holds him back. Ruben is ready for them
both. I can do nothing, I know. I do not fool myself.
Perhaps Danny will return. Marty has Manuel's hands
locked behind him. Behind his drooping eyelids there
is fire. Marty whispers in his ear. "See — ?" he says to
Ruben, angrily. "You got to be a joker, huh? Can't you
let it rest already — you got no sense sometimes, Ruben
baby. None at all." He shakes his head and strains to
hold Manuel. "Easy, Manny boy. Ruben didn't mean
anything. You came on the boat together, remember?
He's your brother, Manny boy. Your brother. Just like
me. I wouldn't lie to you, right?"

Manuel nods.

"He got him in a spell now," Ruben says, turning to
me. He steps backwards and whispers this time, so that
Manuel will not hear. "You know what he do — ? After
you leave, he make him lie down on the subway tracks.
Mi madre, Mister Meyers — I telling you the truth!"

Marty has left Manuel near the window. He has been
listening to us. "You can believe it if you want," he
says. "Between you and me, though, Meyers, it was part
of what we spoke about before, right? Like an initiation."
I do not respond. He is in front of us. "Okay then. Just

answer me this, Ruben — didn't he feel like a king afterwards? Yes or no. Like he was really somebody — ?"
Ruben, I see, grows angrier. It is nothing to me. I put my
shoes on and lace them.

Ruben has not answered. Marty walks away from him,
shaking his head. "Okay, be like that. But answer me
one other thing — who saved him, huh? Who jumped
down in the middle of the tracks with the train coming
in — ?"

"He *loco*, Mister Meyers. He almost kill him. I telling
you — "

I stand and take off my pajama top. There is no need
to take a clean shirt from my dresser. "Come off it, will
you, Ruben? Don't you think I had it all timed — ?" He
glances toward Manuel. "Didn't I save you, Manny boy?"
he asks. Manuel nods his head vigorously. "But you
would have stayed there if I hadn't, right?" Manuel nods
again and it is obvious how proud he is of his bravery.
"Now are you satisfied?" he says to Ruben. "What do you
want to do — take it all away from him?" He lowers his
voice. "I mean, let's face it, what's a kid like that got in
this life, right? Now he feels like somebody."

"You don't got to listen to him," Ruben says to me. "He
get Manuel to do anything he wants now for saving his
life." His mouth is at my ear. "But if they both not here,
Mister Meyers, I tell you the truth about Marty, about why
he got to hide out like me."

Marty puts his hand to his forehead. "Okay. Now I've
heard it all, Ruben baby. You really are shook up, aren't
you?" He sighs. "I guess that stuff with your mother cost
more than we ever figured — "

"*Batardo* — " he hisses. "*Su madre es* — "

"Stay cool, Manny boy," Marty says. He does not even glance his way. Manuel is in a crouch, his eyes on Ruben. He obeys his leader. "Now listen to me for a minute," he says. "You ever hear of the Mandan torture ceremony, Meyers?" I indicate that I have not and he describes it for me. In truth, I am not much interested. He tells me how young Indians are hung by slits which have been cut in their chests. The rawhide is strung to poles over their heads and they stay suspended over the ground from morning until sundown. The entire tribe watches. There are skulls on the ground. I do not listen to all the details. If the young Indian should faint, Marty says, it is proof that he is not a man.

"You don't got to listen," Ruben says.

Marty lowers his voice. "Now let me ask you something, Meyers — and I'm shooting straight with you. You know what Manny's like, right? The way his brain works. So figure this out — if he can't forget about that kind of initiation, do you think he's ever gonna feel good inside about himself?" He stops. "Think about it." His voice is gentle now. I remember what he looked like when I first saw him, crossing the plank between the roofs. He turns to his monkey. "I just can't understand you, Ruben. What do you want to do? Take it all away from him now — ? I mean, what's a kid like that got in this life? We got to work together, baby, don't you know that?" He is pleading with my own monkey, and I think that I believe he means it. "What would you rather have me do once he got that torture stuff on the brain — put him through the real thing?"

"He trying to set Manuel against me, Mister Meyers," Ruben says.

Marty stands. "Look, if you two don't want to come,

it's no skin off me, right? We can always pick up some new joker to collect our money for us — "

"I will come with you," I say.

Ruben looks at me and there is terror in his eyes. I hope you do not tell me what you know about Marty. Everything does not have to be revealed, my monkey. Let us go before Danny returns from work. My decision concerning the telephone was a wise one. I will not even look out the window now to see.

"Okay," Ruben says. "Then I come too."

"That's what I like to hear," Marty says, but as he goes to pat Ruben on the back, my monkey slides away. I let my pajama bottoms drop to the floor and Marty turns his back to me. I step into my trousers. "Don't forget to bring your new doll — we might have time for that mass also — "

Ruben reaches into his side pocket. His fist is in front of Marty's face, but Manuel does not come near them. "You remember I got this," Ruben says. He shows it to Manuel and Manuel moves backwards.

"Sure, Ruben," Marty says. "Sure."

When I have put my jacket and overcoat on, we leave the room. I say nothing about Danny. As we pass Nydia's apartment I hear the downstairs front door open. At the bottom of the stairway Carlos looks up at us. In his arms he carries a bag of groceries. He waits for us to descend.

"They are my students," I explain.

Marty is wary. Manuel waits behind him. "You leave your hands off my wife, man — "

He has set the groceries down on one of the steps. Manuel touches his side pocket. Marty clicks his tongue. "I am an old man," I say.

"And don't you go putting them ideas about school in

her head, mother, or I cut you up good. You got me — ?"

His finger is headed for my chest, but I avoid it. He is bigger and stronger than any of my defenders, I know. For now, though, it is best if he hates me. I do not mind. Ruben is behind him. He and Nydia are the same age. I move directly toward the front door. "Of course," I say, and open the door. I watch Carlos. His face is tired. I hope you are listening, Ruben Fontanez. This is what Harry Meyers was telling you about in the restaurant, don't you see.

"We'll see you around sometime, lover," Marty says to Carlos. "We got to go with our teacher now, right?"

His laughter, I am certain, enrages Carlos, but he leads his two monkeys into the street and Carlos does not follow us. I see the boy in the red baseball cap slip into the abandoned building. That is all right also.

We walk to Broadway and this time we head uptown, past the Lighthouse Nightclub, the Hotel Manhattan Towers, the Daitch Garden Supermarket. The Gitlitz Delicatessen is full. In front of the Apthorpe Apartments a uniformed man holds the door of a taxi open. Further along Broadway I can see the marquee of the old CBS Theater. We stop at 79th Street. Despite the cold, there are many people outside walking. In the Babka Bakery there are still long lines so I know it is not yet dinner hour. To the left, the street slopes toward the Hudson River. The boardwalk, I am sure, is abandoned tonight.

We are in the subway again. "Now there's a couple of things I have to tell you before we get up there," Marty says to me. I look down into the pit where the tracks are and I try to visualize what happened this afternoon. Marty has his arm around Manuel's shoulder. His green bag, I realize, has been left somewhere else. He tells me that he is sure I will understand that they cannot let me know the address. It is not a question of trust. I tell him I understand. When we get to 125th Street, they will have to blindfold me. I nod. We move toward the front end of the station. Manuel's head swivels as he watches an old woman limps by. Her left foot swells monstrously from her shoe. She has elephantiasis, I know, but I do not say the word aloud. Manuel tugs frantically at Marty's sleeve, and Marty tries to reassure him. He praises him again for his bravery in the afternoon. Still, Manuel's eyes follow the woman as she drags herself heavily to a bench. Marty tells me we should not sit together in the subway car, and that if we become separated I am to wait at the northeast corner of 127th Street and Lenox Avenue.

"Now everything this guy will say may not make sense to you — I don't make promises. But I warn you about one thing, Meyers, and I'm giving this to you straight — if you let him know you think he's bats, watch out. Right, Ruben?"

Ruben nods. "You never see anybody so black," he says.

"And that's another thing," Marty says. "Don't say anything about his skin. He — " A downtown express train rattles through the middle row of tracks. I see the red lights of our own train entering at the rear of the station. I do not hear Marty's further instructions, though I nod assent to them.

In the subway I take a seat near the middle doors and I close my eyes. I should have eaten something before we left. I do not need to look at the people around me. College students are in the majority. I wish them well, also. At 96th Street I follow my three boys across the platform to the 145th Street Lenox Avenue Line. The faces in the car are black. They are all tired. It is not Friday, I know, or they would be talking of pay envelopes. I wonder if the Italian baths are still in use at the far east end of Harlem. I will tell you something: Harry Meyers voted for Vito Marcantonio for Mayor in 1948. A Negro policeman walks through our car, but he does not glance at my three boys. Nobody talks. Nobody reads newspapers. If we did not have to get off at various stops, we would all be sleeping, I am sure.

My glands are more active than they were earlier in the day. Perhaps we will be able to stop for a drink before we visit the old man. I do not consider inviting him to my room. I do not worry about Mrs. Wenger. I will encourage Morris no longer. I will tell Danny and he will have no choice but to honor my wish. He would not fight with me, I am certain. At 125th Street we get out of the train and wait under the arcade for all the people to pass us. Manuel gives Marty a black scarf and I stoop down so that he can tie it around my eyes. In Harlem, Marty assures me, nobody will think twice about such things.

The noises of cars and radios surround us. "You hold on to me," Ruben says and I let him take me by the hand. In truth, the sounds are not so different from those on the West Side. I am not much interested in seeing 125th Street. I have been here before. The noise slackens and I know we are on a side street. The pressure of Ruben's hand is firm and I do not stumble once, even when I step up and down from the curbs.

"We told him all about you already," Marty says. "Just in case. He says he heard of you, what you did that time — "

"What is his name?" I ask.

"We call him Old York. Nobody knows his real name, though," Marty says. I hear the screams of cats. "He's supposed to be descended from the original York — the jig who was Clark's slave on the Lewis and Clark expedition. I'm not saying yes, I'm not saying no — "

"He has the spots also," Ruben whispers to me. He tugs gently at my hand and I know I must step up. "That is why Marty — "

"Cool it, Ruben," Marty says. His voice is tense. "You're really asking for it, aren't you? You really want me to sic Manny on you one of these first days, don't you?"

"He ruled an island in South America," Ruben says.

Marty has decided it is not the time to lecture Ruben. He holds his anger back and tells me that what my monkey says may be the reason we cannot learn his real name. He speaks impatiently. He suspects that the name of Old York is merely a cover-up, so that the enemies who followed him in his exile could not find and kill him. "You believe what you want, Meyers," he said. "It's nothing to me one way or the other."

Our steps echo quietly along the street. People no longer pass us. There are brownstones here also, I know. The scarf has loosened somewhat and when I look down I can see under it to the sidewalk. Without my glasses on, though, it is all a blur. I do not hear Manuel's footsteps. "We're gonna have to leave the blindfold on till we get inside his room — so he'll know," Marty says. I smell sour milk and my stomach is uneasy. Ruben tells me that we are going up steps and I hold on to his hand more tightly as I walk with him. We are in a building. I smell the odors of urine and frying bacon. It is warmer. I am very

G

dizzy. "I have the doll — " Ruben begins, but I hear Marty hit him on the side of his head. My monkey staggers. "Shut up!" Marty says. "How many times do I have to tell you to stop talking so much?" Ruben's hand drops from mine and I move my own hands to the blindfold. I am ready, you see. I would try to stop Manuel. I know it.

"Man, you scared shitless," Ruben says. I do not hear Manuel. I stick a thumb under the blindfold. "It's okay, Mister Meyers," Ruben says, and he takes my hand again. "I not going to fight them." I wonder if he knew what I was thinking. I cannot see his face. "I no mean nothing, Manuel," he says. There is new life in his voice. His leader is not in complete control any longer, you see.

The wooden steps creak under us. Spots or no spots, he is merely an old man, I tell myself. If it gives him pleasure to play games with children, that is his business. As for Harry Meyers, the games are already over. He lets his monkey lead him now only because it is less difficult this way. I do not think he fools himself about that. To break suddenly after what has happened would cause infinite complications. I am certain of it. There will be time to take care of things when our visit is completed. And you need not worry about me, Marty. I will not respond to anything your leader says. We have stopped. If I judge correctly, we are at the third landing. Marty is listening. He tells Manuel to put out his cigarette. I am surprised at how tense he is. Perhaps, I think, perhaps you too are only a boy, Marty. I think this even while I remember what you have done to Manuel today.

"You sure you want to go through with this, Meyers?" Marty whispers. His voice is tight. I know what Ruben would like me to say, but I know better. I nod my head.

"Okay then," Marty says. I tilt my head back and, under my blindfold, I can see Marty's hand gripping my own monkey's arm. "And you keep your trap shut about this afternoon, hear? I'll tell him when it's time." He wipes his mouth. "You trust me, right, Manny boy?" I do not have to look at Manuel to know what his answer is. "Old York will really be proud of you. You'll see —"

Then he knocks on the door, three times in quick succession. There is no response. He knocks again, four times, pausing between each rap on the wood. I remember you scratching at my door, Ruben Fontanez, and I do not envy you your dream. The door opens and Marty enters first, with Manuel. Ruben takes my hand and I follow him inside. The door closes. The air is heavy and the odor is like that in the *Genizah* where my cowboys leave all their decaying books and scrolls. Even when it is no longer of use, my cowboys believe that you are not allowed to destroy a book. It is a law a teacher can appreciate. "Sit here," Ruben says, and I rest in a wooden chair. There is another odor also, sweeter, like that of orange peels boiling.

"This is Harry Meyers," Marty says. "We kept him blindfolded —"

I hear somebody grunt. A chair scrapes. At the cuffs of my trousers a soft shape brushes against me. "Okay," Marty says from behind me and he unties the knot. I take my glasses out of my pocket, but they do not help much. The room is black. Ruben is to my left, sitting in a chair. Manuel and Marty are to my right. In front of me a match is struck against what sounds like stone and for an instant I see the face that Ruben has spoken of. It is dry and black and the pits of the eyes are deep. So. There were black Indians also. I believe you, Marty. The man's body is obscured by a broad flat table. A candle is lit beneath his face now, in a glass bowl. On one corner of the table I see a stack of narrow books like those my father kept his accounts in. "It has been written," the old man says, and the voice does not frighten me at all. It is weak and scratchy. The shape that brushed at my legs leaps lightly onto my lap. I see light in its two green eyes and I stroke its fur. When we were first married, we had a cat, but it was killed by a car on Eastern Parkway and Sarah would not get another. Well. Things will not be so terrible, after all. I will stay for the performance. I will let my young guardians blindfold me again. When we return home I will tell them that Danny came by this afternoon. I will tell them what he said and then we will separate. The cat purrs and, with my fingers under its throat, I can feel its body vibrate.

The old man stands and he is taller than I thought. His back is not bent. He mutters and makes mysterious motions in the air. My own monkey can do as well, I think. I remember standing in Williamsburg, in the cold, with the men from the building moving toward me. But that is all right also, my monkey. When you tell me you meant nothing, I will believe you. It does not matter now. From the floor beside him the old man lifts something heavy and white. He wraps it around his shoulders.

Marty is talking. He says that the cape is made from the skin of a white buffalo. There is only one in five million. He does not sound like my young rebel. His voice is soft and even. The old man laughs, but his cackling does not disturb me. It is harmless. I scratch the cat behind its ears and it takes my fingers in its mouth and chews gently. It wants the sides of its jaw rubbed. One paw rests across my wrist. Marty talks of regiments of Negro cavalry which the

Indians called black buffaloes. Ruben waits quietly. The light from the candle shows me things hanging from the walls that look like shrunken heads, but I am not much interested. I have seen my students reading the comic books and catalogues. In a corner of the room, behind the old man, I see his bed. It is neatly made, and he has it covered with a khaki army blanket. To the right, I see a gas burner and a refrigerator. The refrigerator is much smaller than my own. I smile. Perhaps, I think, Morris could interest you also.

The old man is speaking to Marty now. He seems to be embarrassed by my presence. He sucks on his lips and I realize that what makes his words so difficult to understand is the absence of teeth. I squint but I cannot find the outlines of lips. I look to the right and see that Marty's mouth is half open. His eyes do not waver. Manuel leans sideways with his head against his leader's shoulders. You could have shared a room at the farm. Marty would have tutored you, Manuel. There was one time, I remember, when I did something about my proposal, though even I knew how futile it was. "Knives and guns, my friend," Old York is saying. "My children are waiting under the city. Give me the money."

My cowboys, I am certain, would not be taken in by such talk. But when Marty stands I realize that he is under a spell as deep as the one he holds over his own monkey. He takes his beret from his head. "They'll never get me, right. No matter how much money my old man gives to those bastards, right?"

"It has been written," Old York says. He lets dust fall through his fingers to the table. The flame sizzles and glows more brightly. I suppose I felt guilty, Sarah, at having abandoned our plans. So I did what you hinted I should do. I sigh. It was all so absurd and I can shrug it off now, but it is something I have not wanted to think about. Well. It is all right.

Marty reaches under his shirt and pours coins into the beret. It is the money they have earned from their performances. I cannot concentrate on the dialogue that goes on between them. I took the insurance money, you see, and went to the real estate man and we drove upstate together. I did not give him my real name. I told no teachers, no brothers, not even Morris. Old York swings something above his head and the cat leaps onto the table and tries to strike it with its paws. "This is what happens, my friend," he says to me, and I can see the pinkness inside his mouth. He takes the cat by the back of the neck and throws it into a corner, against the wall. Its cry does not bother me. Old York talks of what happens to those who betray him.

"At the place," Marty says, "they kept trying to get me to confess I tried to kill my old man — but I never told them anything." Old York nods his approval. Marty talks on, making vague threats about what will happen next time. Well. It is not so easy to be the youngest son. "They play God," Marty says. "I had it all figured out, right? Those jokers didn't fool me. You confess you need help and then they tell you everything's okay. Just trust them and they'll save you — " The cat sits on the bed now, licking a paw and cleaning itself. If a woman is scared by a cat while she carries a child, my cowboys believe, she will give birth to a monster. Still, I will return to them on Monday.

I am tired, though. I would not be unhappy if we left now, but I remember Marty's instructions. Let things run their course, Harry. The old man smiles at his young disciple and assures him he will remain free. His eyes will not meet mine. He is reminding Marty of the spots they share, of things he has done for him, of his power. The black Jews of Abyssinia were called Falashos. The Muslims were kind to them. In his lap, Ruben holds his new doll. Along my right shoulder, between my neck and the joint of my arm, a muscle pulses lightly under the skin, out of control. I touch it. It quivers for an instant and then ceases. The room seems very still. The muscles alongside my throat are tight. My friendly gland responds to my touch. When I arrived at the farm with the real estate man, I did not want to get out of the car. The supervisor had been correct. The idea was unoriginal, unworkable. And without Sarah, of course, there was not adequate desire. Still, I walked around the premises, the owner in front of us, keeping up a pace which quickly tired me. He called me "Pop," I remember. "You take your time, Pop, and let me know what you think," he said to me. I smiled nervously and let the real estate man engage in deliberations. The owner was returning to his family in Illinois, to a larger farm, one he could work with his two sons.

I leave my throat alone and remind myself that it would not be a bad idea to check with the doctor before Monday. These last few days have not been uneventful. The old man is pointing at me now and he stands in front of the table.

"*Mi madre*," Ruben says softly. "You got to watch out, Mister Meyers."

His breath is terrible and with the candle behind him I cannot get a good look at his face. "You know how old I am, Pop?" the man asked me. I said I did not. He seemed to be in the prime of his life. He was friendly, easy-going. His hair was thin, but still golden, with some white patches around his ears. "Guess how old I am — " Before I left he told me. "I'll be sixty-two in another month, Pop," he said proudly. "You believe it?"

I said I did, though it seemed impossible. Well. People have different lives. I was not even close to sixty at the time. Your energy will be gone someday also, Marty. Your schemes will disappear. When you and Manuel are separated, who will you get to listen to your stories? Old York's eyes are veined and his body, I see, is very thin. I would not like to guess at his age. When you are no longer a boy, my young rebel, the steel men will not be interested in you. "Give me the money," he says. "The dollar bills also — "

"It's all we got," Marty says. "Cross my heart — " I have enough saved, I know. I will be all right. "They won't get me, right?"

"Give me the money." I felt guilty toward the real estate man, I recall. He was cheerful all the way back to the city, and I promised to call the next day. He trusted me.

"Give me the money."

"Don't you use these boys!" The words come from the mouth of Harry Meyers. I am standing and I try to stop Marty from giving his money away. My efforts are clumsy. The coins splatter to the floor. The cat leaps from the bed, chasing the noises. "They are flesh also! Do you hear me?" The sides of my fists pound against the old man's chest. It is flat, like a board, and he falls back at once. I have seen my boys at work. They are entitled also.

The old man's fur cape swirls behind him. I move forward once more. I am not so tired, it seems. "Do you hear me — ?"

"Aiee, Mister Meyers — " Ruben says. "Watch out! What you gone to do?"

Reaching backwards, Old York knocks over the candle, but it does not go out. The glass bowl rocks on its side, next to the ledger books. I hear a hissing sound and know who is ready for me. I should have considered such things first. Harry, Harry. In my hand I hold Marty's beret. I look at him and see the band of silver that presses his teeth into a uniform arc. The old man tries to talk but my fists have done good work. I can see Jackson, standing in the snow.

"Get him, Manny," Marty whispers.

"*Bruja,* Manuel — " My monkey steps between us, his fist raised above his head. He tears open the envelope and clutches the earth. "The door, Mister Meyers," he says, and I do not hesitate. He knows what he is doing, I realize. He has not had Harry Meyers as a teacher for nothing. The old man holds something long and silver in his right hand. He has not yet caught his breath, though. My own hands tremble. My stomach is unsettled. I feel very tired again.

"It's bunk, Manny boy. Get him — " Marty's old voice has returned.

"*Bruja,* Manuel," Ruben says again. "*¡Bruja!* From the grave of my mother. She will protect us — "

The old man hesitates. The cat is on the table, leaping for what the old man holds in his right hand. The edge is silver. I should have left earlier. Who knows what your life has been like, old man. I am not so angry any longer. Marty whispers to his own monkey. Ruben stands in front of me. I hear the hissing sound again and see the blade clearly. It is too late. My hand is on the doorknob. "*¡Bruja! ¡Bruja!*" Ruben says. He is directly in front of

G*

me. *"Mi madre, sálvenos — "* he cries, and he throws the dirt at the old man's table.

Manuel retreats. From the table, though I know at once that there must be ordinary explanations, there is a sizzling sound and a puff of smoke. "Aiee — " Ruben cries. The old man covers his eyes. I do not look twice. "Now, Mister Meyers," Ruben says, and I pull the door open. *"¡Mi madre — !"* he shouts over his shoulder as we head down the dark stairway. Under my fingers the wood of the bannister is like satin.

"The blindfold?" I ask when we are in the street.

"Oh man," Ruben says. "This no time to make jokes, Mister Meyers. He tell the truth when he talk about all his children — he got lots of guys like us working for him under the city. Like I told you — "

He grabs my hand and pulls me toward the corner. I see the shapes of cats moving among swollen garbage pails. I smell wine. "We in good trouble now. I telling you — "

"How is Manuel's sister?" I ask.

His fingers dig through my overcoat, my jacket, my shirt. "Aiee, you *loco* also — " He yanks at my arm. "What I gone to *do,* Mister Meyers? What I gone to *do* — ?"

The sign above us says 131st Street and Lenox Avenue. The cars speed by. I see no policemen. I look for a red baseball cap. Ruben's eyes glance behind us but the street is still empty. I hope the old man is all right. Harlem Hospital is nearby, though, if my memory serves me correctly. I will give you a choice, Ruben Fontanez, before I return the magazine article to the school. Perhaps you would like it for yourself. Well. Perhaps you were right. Harry Meyers may not be so old, after all. Who would have suspected such anger, such strength? If no rumors accompany me concerning these last few days, the students will whisper about Mad-Man Meyers once more. I am certain of it.

"The subway," Ruben is saying. "It's our only chance." I let him lead me along Lenox Avenue. We move uptown this time. "I know them all by heart," he says to me. "We get the Flushing train out to Queens. Then maybe we switch for the GG to Brooklyn." I do not look at the houses, or the stores, or the cars, or the people who pass us. Nor do I look behind. I leave such things to my monkey. Danny would have been proud of me. "I know hiding places in the tunnels, where the workmen stay — " Some young boys sit in front of an abandoned store, waiting to shine people's shoes. One of them approaches me and I tell him that I have no need of his services.

"But man, your shoes real dirty — " he says. His face is round and one of his cheeks is raw under the brown skin, as if it has been in a fire. He follows us to the corner of 134th Street, carrying his wooden stand. "You sure you don't want a shine? Just ten cents, mister." He skips in front of us and makes a pass at my shoes with his cloth. "How you wear such dirty shoes, man?"

Ruben shoves him aside. "Get lost, kid — " he says. "*Váyate.*"

"Up yours, mother," the young boy says, but Ruben has no time to engage him in conversation. He pulls me along after him. "Hey man, your shoes eat it — !" the boy calls after me. I turn my head back and smile. "You a real fag-ass — "

We are at the entrance but I will go no further. I have had enough subways for one day. "Come," I say. "We will take a taxi — " My monkey's body straightens. His eyes show that he is relieved. They are gray again, tending toward brown at the edges. It is the least I can do for him. I wonder what it was that Manuel did to earn his keep before Marty came to his aid. Ruben has already found a taxi for us. It is yellow and orange and the door is held open for me. I do not need to apologize to Ruben for what he calls my jokes. He understands.

"West 76th Street," I say to the driver. "Between Amsterdam and Columbus avenues."

Ruben sits beside me and looks out the side window. The driver makes a U turn around the island in the middle of the avenue and heads downtown. I close my eyes. "They be coming there pretty soon," Ruben says. "We got to think of something. Old York gone to get all his men after us — " He shakes his head sideways. "Why you do it, Mister Meyers?"

I look at my monkey. It would be too much trouble if I were to begin. I am too tired for long explanations now. I shrug. I think of telling him that I had no choice, but I am not sure he would understand. It would only mean more questions. "Danny will call the police," I say, and while I am saying the words, I know, of course, what they mean for my monkey.

He says nothing. The driver is listening to a basketball game on the radio. Well. It is true that you would be safe there, with your brothers and sisters, but that is not, after all, the way we would like things to turn out, is it. What you do about it is your own business, my monkey. You can leave when you want. "I did not do so much," I say.

"You do enough," Ruben says, and for the first time

this evening, he laughs. "Aiee — you *loco* sometimes, Mister Meyers. I never know anybody like you — "

I did not do so much. Still, I try to remember what has happened. Ruben shakes his head. He tells me again that he has never known anybody like me. My chest feels heavy. I suppose that I have been more active than I would care to admit. I do not, in fact, recall going down the staircase in the building. I can see the puff of smoke, though. I hear Manuel. All right, Ruben. All right. I will ask you no questions now. But before we are finished, believe me, Harry Meyers will know. The name of our driver is Gerardo Luis Morales and I wonder how many children he has, though I will not ask about that either. I leave the windows to you, Ruben Fontanez. The city does not interest me much.

The doll is in your lap now, and two pins pierce it. My mind must have been wandering. I should pay closer attention. But it is all right. Marty concerns me no longer. I worry about Manuel, though. "It be better if we get out a few blocks from home," Ruben says. "You let me go ahead of you, in case — " I nod. Ruben tells the driver where to stop. We are crossing Manhattan island now, through Central Park. The trees are bare. There are no people walking. I see no shadows. I wonder again about the things Jackson actually did during the three days.

Harry, Harry, I tell myself. Stop. It will all be over soon. In the long run it will be for the best. Danny will survive. Remember what has just happened. In truth, you could not go through another dinner. Do not fool yourself. We are out of the park. A dog trots in front of our taxi and our driver curses. The meter reads $1.35. Ruben slopes forward on the seat, touching the doll, look-

ing to both sides of the street. We have stopped on West
End Avenue, across from the Collegiate Church. The
meter reads $1.55 and I give the driver two dollar bills
and do not accept any change. But my own monkey is out
of the taxi before the transaction is completed and he does
not know. The driver pulls the door closed behind me
and does not say thank you. Still, he does not seem to
question the fact of whom I ride with, and that is something. I wish him well also.

"You stay behind me," Ruben says. "We got to be careful."

"They could not have gotten here before us," I say.

Ruben nods. "I want to go upstairs first. I got to tell
your friend Danny something," he says. "Then we come
down together and take care of things with you — "

I thank him for thinking of saving me the four flights
up and down. I am not sure I am up to it. He tells me to
shout to him if I suspect anything, and then we part.
When he is almost at Broadway, I begin following.

The brownstones on this side of Broadway are more
various than those on my own block, I must admit. Their
top floors give the appearance of castles. Across Broadway
the candy store is empty. People wait in the laundromat.
There is a new display in the window of the G & S Linen
Store. I do not look at the faces of the people who pass
me. My shoes do not pinch my toes as they did earlier today. In all my years on the West Side, I realize, I have
never eaten in the Tibbs Wharf Restaurant. In front of
the Hotel Manhattan Towers a sign tells me when bingo
will be played. I turn left. Cars fill the street, returning to their apartment house garages and rental agencies.
I cannot say I dislike living here, but I am certain that
living without winter for one year would not be terrible.

Overhead I hear the sound of an electric guitar. Behind me there are steps but I do not bother to look. As I have told you, I am ready. In front of me, a half block beyond Amsterdam Avenue I see the shapes moving toward him. I do not think any are taller than he is. Old York told the truth about his children. I stop to watch. Unless Marty and Manuel are with them they will not recognize me, I know. The circle is closing. A number 11 bus passes in front of me.

I am right. My monkey will lead them away from me. His head bobs from side to side. His feet dance in the pavement. Then he is gone, away from the hands of his adversaries, streaking between cars, leaping toward Columbus Avenue. If others do not wait for him at the edge of Central Park, he will escape. I remember how his feet moved in the classroom when he held my likeness in his hand. Still, he may get tired. I do not know if he has eaten anything since his lunch break. And all the money is somewhere else. But this is not the time to think of what could happen to you, Ruben Fontanez. I am sorry. Harry Meyers must look out for himself. The light is green and I cross Amsterdam Avenue. The dark shapes are gone. I see nothing before me and do not, in fact, recall seeing anyone chase my monkey. It is his decision. It will be less difficult if I am alone with Danny. Ruben has assured me that he knows the secret passageways of the New York City subway system. I cross over to my side of the street and look up at the roofs, but my monkey is not there. There are no steps behind me. No men come from the synagogue. The street is free of cars.

I am almost home. I hum to myself. In Nydia's apartment, I see, there is a light. I step down and put my hand on the doorknob and then I hear the breathing. The red cap rises from behind the garbage pails and I see the gold tooth. There is nothing to do, I realize. "I told you, man," a voice says, and it comes toward me. The strength that rose up against Old York is gone. It would be useless to think otherwise. It has been a long day and I must admit that I have not been well lately. "Can't wait — " The words are blurred. My hand stays on the doorknob. His breath smells of cheap wine. I try not to think of the scene in the gardens. If I could ring the bell perhaps Danny would come down. It would be foolish to try Carlos. First, he says, he wants my money. Something cold and silver is at my throat, but I do not think I am frightened. I reach into my pocket for my wallet.

"Get him, Manny — "

I turn my head in time to see my smallest monkey leap over the garbage cans and land on my assailant's back. I push open the door and press my finger on Harry Meyers' buzzer. I step back into the shadows and watch. I see the black face, but there is no baseball cap now. I do not wish to see the struggle. I hear a hissing sound. Another shape comes near. Marty looks at me through the glass door and smiles. I hear his instructions.

"It's yours, Manny boy — the way I taught you — "

The knife rises in the air and I turn my head away. The scream I hear an instant later is like nothing human. It moves through me and I fall forward against the mailboxes, unable to support my body. What little food is left moves upwards and in my mouth I taste the bile. My hands tremble, the muscle in my neck twitches, I breathe quickly. The scream reverberates in my skull and, in truth, I wish it were all over.

"The cops, Manny — *la jora* — !" My guardian's eyes

look through the glass door, appealing to me. My mouth
hangs open. I will not look down at what has been accomplished. *"La jora,* Manny! Come on." He pleads with
his own monkey. He does not want to desert him, I
know. "The cops, damn it. Enough —"

Then he is gone. He had no choice, after all. I am glad
I did not hear everything he and Old York said to one another. There are only two figures outside the door now,
but more descend upon us instantly. It is difficult for
me to stay awake. People have different lives. I would not
ask anybody to guess my age. I hear sirens and shouts. I
see a club fall. I see light flash from silver badges. My
knees have given way. I am truly sorry, I will tell you
that. The door opens and someone takes me under the
arms and supports me.

"I got him —" Danny says, and he loosens my collar.
Then he speaks with a great gentleness. "C'mon, Mister
Meyers. No need for you to look. Let's get you upstairs
and we'll have the doc here in a few minutes." Another
figure is beside me but Danny says he can manage alone. I
touch his hand with mine and want to tell him that I will
be all right. "I had a hunch," he says. "You know what I
mean? There was something about that spic kid I didn't
trust. A good thing too." We are in the lobby where it is
very warm and thick. Nydia rocks her baby in her arms.
Carlos asks if he can help. You are too harsh sometimes,
Harry. Danny continues to talk to me as we ascend. "It's
a good thing we had a tail put on them. Dear Christ,
Mister Meyers, you don't know what that kid did — in
my wildest dreams —" He stops himself and wipes my
forehead with a handkerchief. "You wanna rest a minute?"

I nod and we stop at the third landing. Nobody joins us. They must be looking from their windows. The hospital is nearby. I was right, you see, to have been concerned about Manuel. I wonder what they will do to him. I lean against Danny and take some more steps. My strength returns more quickly than I might have expected. But four flights is insane for a man my age. "The whole back of the guy's head was just — "

"Stop — " It is the best I can do. "Please." I must swallow several times. I know full well, believe me. So, we have followed one another through the city, after all, I think. Harry Meyers behind his monkey and Marty and Manuel behind Harry Meyers and Danny and his police behind us all. It was not the kind of chain I had in mind. I am sorry. Do you hear me? I am sorry. I do not know how else to say it. My right hand begins to shake uncontrollably. I press it down with my left one and Danny pretends that he does not see. I am very dizzy. It will not be any easier now, I know. I wish the sirens would stop. Danny says he will get the key from my pocket. He is angry suddenly, and if I could, I would tell him that, in truth, I did not know the doll had been placed in the side pocket of my overcoat.

"Dumb kids," he says, and, in fury, he hurls his likeness down the stairs. The sound is soft. If I had the strength I would warn him. But it is too late. The pins are still there. I am certain of it. My door opens. The room is dark. If I were to pull the window shades up I think I know what I would see on the rooftop across the street. One of the sirens is leaving us. "I'm just glad for one thing," Danny says. "That you didn't get a look, Mister Meyers. I had a hunch, you know what I mean — ?"

EIGHT

It is morning again. I sit at my desk, drinking tea and arranging my books. Danny is gone, his suitcase with him. I do not need to look out my window to know what passes in the street below me. I do not need to look across at the abandoned buildings. The wreckers can have you, Sarah. I am sorry. They can have anything they want now, I suppose. It is nothing to me. I put on my galoshes to protect the bottoms of my trousers. It has been snowing all weekend. Marty's green bag rests next to the fireplace, but I am not expecting him to return. He is not so foolish. There is other territory for him, I am certain. I place the magazine article in my briefcase, between the Hebrew books. I will leave it in the biology teacher's mailbox. Ruben need not know. Let the children see, though. It would be of little use to place it in the garbage can downstairs. After all, that is not the lost treasure you seek, old woman.

I am still tired, but there is no longer any reason to stay in my room. Except for Morris and Nydia I would have no visitors. If there is time, perhaps it is Harry Meyers who should begin talking to Morris. I could persuade him. He knows that I have enough savings for both of us. We could live without winters. All the years in this city have not made us love them. He is entitled to a trip also. Perhaps his home would give him a refund. If not, he could try to sell his bed to another. Harry Meyers could recommend somebody. I zip my briefcase closed, sip the last of the tea, and put on my overcoat. Despite everything, my body is free of aches. The hot baths the last two nights were a true pleasure. I should take them more often. My throat feels relaxed this morning. I smooth the blankets back across my bed and smile at my likeness on the night table. There is no need to take it with me. It is at home here. There is nothing else to do. I go out and close the door behind me.

Behind the other doors, there are no sounds. On the staircase there is no trace of what Danny threw away. When he complained of pains in his chest, there was nothing for Harry Meyers to say to him. He laughed, of course, and said that he would have to take things more easily at night. There are ordinary explanations, I know. He spoke of his beer belly, of running with the police, of sleeping on his side in my easy chair, of working overtime at his factory, and, at some length, of a new woman friend of his. He winked at me many times. He was certain we understood one another. He assured me that what was happening had nothing to do with Jean, whom he loved dearly. She was the mother of little Gil, he reminded me. Still, as he had told me before, it was not natural for a man to lie in one bed with one woman for an entire lifetime.

I lay in my own bed and I listened to him. I said nothing. His descriptions of his new pleasures merged with his recounting of what had happened downstairs. It took three policemen to subdue Manuel, and Danny marveled at his strength. His new friend, he tells me, is demanding. He envies Manuel's energy. I stop in front of Nydia's door, but I hear nothing. Carlos is a good husband. It would be unfair to give his wife false hopes. There are rules and regulations in this world, and Harry Meyers is not about to start a campaign against the Board of Education. I am afraid you have lost your chance, Nydia. It is too late, you see. But you have your child, and a husband, and you live in a heated building. There are not many fifteen-year-old Puerto Rican girls in New York City who can say the same thing. Education is not everything. What I have said to my own monkey does not apply in all times and places.

I do not hesitate to pass through the downstairs hallway or the front lobby. There will be no more notes in my mailbox. It is cold outside. I glance to my right and see some men in front of the synagogue. They shake hands with each other. If they wish to put their hearts as well as their minds into their prayers, that is their business. If they mock the newcomers, that is all right also. It is nothing to me. I walk past the Park West Hospital. Behind the glass door a blond-haired nurse smiles at me. I nod to her. The doorman across the street blows into his hands to warm them. The sidewalks have all been salted. A wall of snow surrounds most of the cars, but the street itself is cleared for passage. I see no light on in the abandoned building. I do not look at the roofs. No limousines wait outside the Riverside Chapel. I continue straight to Broadway this morning. I can be a few minutes late. I do not wish to talk to all the teachers, to know if the story of my new adventure has circulated yet. Danny said there were photographers. If they wanted pictures of Harry Meyers this time, though, they would have to go into their back files to get them.

They were not the last pictures, Danny assured me. He waits patiently for the day of Jackson's release. So. You have helped me there also, my smallest monkey. When he marveled at what you had done I reminded him that I no longer needed protection. I gave him a choice, you see: if he wished to persist in his plan, Harry Meyers would no longer visit him. I am an old man, I said. He nodded, and once more he recalled for me what had happened so many years ago in the snow. He understood how I felt, he told me. It would be less than true to say I gave him the choice with the hope of sparing Jackson, but that had some small part in it. Still, I think I knew what his answer would be. I have been, it seems, only the second most important man in his life.

Across Broadway the men carry armfuls of fish into Citarella's. I can see the baked goods in the window of the Tiptoe Inn. I stop to admire the intricate shadows that rise upwards on the walls of the Ansonia Hotel. There was something in our parting which troubled me. I admit it. Though my feelings were short of tears, his were genuine. It was a choice he made with much pain, though with little difficulty, I suspect. And he understood that it was final, unless he changes his mind about Jackson. I have little to worry about. What he tells Jean is his business. If I understood him correctly, he may tell her nothing for a while. Harry Meyers can serve as an alibi for his other visits. Well. That is all right also. The important thing has been accomplished. It is too late for anything more.

On this side of Verdi Square a middle-aged man sleeps on his side, stretched out under the *New York Times*. There is a bluish tint to his unshaven face. At the subway station, the deaf news deliverers wait in silence for the next truck. I have no need to purchase tokens this morning. I took care of that the other night. The platform is crowded and I take my place near the front, trying not to look into anyone's face. Without my subway three, these trips will be an ordeal, I know. It will be best to let them pass without noticing things. The hot air from blowers makes my stomach turn. Two old women, their faces black, lean against one another. They spend their days cleaning other people's homes. From their workshoes I see the white cotton socks, the tops stretched. A Puerto Rican woman, a few years older than Nydia, tries to stop her baby from crying while four other children crowd around her skirt. They all suck their thumbs. A subway man moves sluggishly between us, emptying the trash tins under the candy machines. As the train fills the well in front of us, I notice the stream of water that flows between the tracks. I sit across from the five children and wonder who will tell Manuel the story of the sewer babies now. The train slams from side to side and I have slight trouble balancing myself. I do not look at the headlines of the newspapers around me. I can smell liver sausage. I think I hear the sound of Old York's cat, its throat rumbling softly under my fingertips. I close my eyes.

At the Delancey Street station I get out and walk past

the pretzel man and the doughnut counter to the BMT line. My timing has been perfect. No other teachers are waiting. I board the train. We leave Manhattan island. From the Williamsburg Bridge I see the river moving coldly beneath me. The train is only half full but I stand by the middle door. Smoke rises above the snow, from the shoreline. No barges move on the water. In the distance I see the dome of the Williamsburg Savings Bank. The swift crisscrossing of steel girders on either side of our subway car makes me dizzy and I look down. My shoes do not pinch today. I will be able to teach standing up. No doubt there will already be a substitute teacher to take my place, but they can find other things for him to do. Let them arrange the records however they want. It is nothing to me. With such weather, though, I can count on a shortage.

There is a thin coat of ice above the planks of the Marcy Street platform. Well. I am here again. I wonder if the remaining few months will equal in length all the years that have preceded them. I will tell you this: Harry Meyers will try to teach his students something. It has nothing to do with you, Sarah, I can assure you. I step down from the green exit onto the slush-filled sidewalk. My galoshes give me sure footing. My briefcase is not very heavy. Two young men, their eyes ringed with sleeplessness, stand behind the counter deep-frying the food that reminds them of their origins. The Rancho Luna Luncheonette has been here for many years, and the help has changed with the seasons. From my appearance they would not suspect that I can understand their words. The windows are half steamed. I will not go inside. Do you know what I can remember — ? The times Morris and I would watch the old cowboy movies and catch the moments when the actors who portrayed the Indians would ad lib in Yiddish. I smile. It is a pleasant memory. The Chassidim are already engaged in their daily commerce. They go in and out of banks and real estate offices, but they do not look at me. They carry briefcases also, and the bottoms of their black kaftans are wet from the snow. I could tell Morris that he is right: they will be invading the West Side soon. They stay away from the warmer climates. It would make a convincing argument.

Harry, Harry, I tell myself. Forget it. There is no time for such adventures. What you do, do by yourself. The games are over. I cross the street, toward the Brooklyn-Queens Expressway. I do not read the scribbling on the bricks of the underpass. I step on clean snow and I hear the skin of ice crystals crack under my galoshes. The shadow I see does not disturb me.

"Mister Meyers — " It is my own monkey, whispering, and he has been waiting on the other side of the underpass. I stop. My heart beats more quickly. Light glints from his misshapen forehead. His sneakers tread through the puddles of melting snow. Under his jacket there is only a T-shirt. But his eyes, I see, his eyes are still the eyes of a cowboy. "I knew you be coming back today!" he says, and I know at once that I am happy to see him again, glad that I have not disappointed him. I can find no words, but I think my smile tells him what I am feeling. He beckons with his finger and I follow him into a corner, where it is darker. "I got to watch out for the cops — they really after us now," he says. "But I want to see you one more time before I go. To tell you — "

"I am glad," I say. I put my briefcase down in a spot that has stayed dry.

Ruben's eyes move from side to side. "Listen: I want you to know I didn't run out on you then — "

"I know," I say.

"Okay," he says. "Listen: I want you to know that we not going to let Manuel stay where he is forever. We gone to spring him someday, Mister Meyers, if it the last thing we do!" He twists his head toward me and his eyes are not the eyes of a boy any longer. I was right about that also, you see. He could not work in the subways many more months. He grows too quickly. He will need new clothes. "He give his life for us — "

I nod. My hands stay in my pockets. "Okay," Ruben says. "Now listen: I want you to know you don't got to worry about me. I watch out for myself. They not gone to get me, Mister Meyers. We got some good places to hole out in now — and soon they stop looking for us." He shakes his head sideways. "There one bad thing, though." I look into his eyes. "Manuel's sister."

"I am sorry," I say.

"She really flip her lid when she hear," he says. "I wish I can do something, but — " He shrugs, helplessly. I tell him again that I am sorry. He tells me that she has been pouring gasoline on the dolls she has saved since childhood. Nobody can reason with her. Every day she burns another doll and Ruben does not know where it will end. Manuel was her brother. I tell my monkey that if he sees her he should tell her how grateful I am to Manuel. I realize that, in truth, Danny did not save me. I suppose that means that we are even at last. I smile. Remember: I am the man who did not save Danny's son. It is a curious thought and I do not dwell upon it. My own monkey, I see, is restless. I do not want to keep him. He vows again that he and Marty will free Manuel someday. They work together again, it seems, and I make no comment. Ruben does not ask for my approval and that is just as well.

"The boy that Manuel — " I begin. "He is still alive."

"I glad on that," Ruben says. "I telling you the truth, Mister Meyers." Wind whips through the underpass suddenly and I turn my back against its force. Ruben covers his eyes. "Listen," he says. "I bring something I want to show you." He reaches under his jacket, to his waist, and takes out a brown grocery bag. "I bringing this to his sister now. I gone to meet her somewhere — I not stupid enough to go where she lives. They be waiting for us to come there. But we got a place to meet. She knows." He opens the bag. Inside, I see, are hundreds of photographs, all of them the same size. "Every day Marty give him a quarter from what we make and he go into one of the booths in the subway to take four pictures of himself." I look at several of the photographs. They are all alike. In each, Manuel faces straight into the camera, unsmiling, sleepy-eyed. "I got more bags filled," Ruben says. "Where we hiding out. I give them all to Mara before we go." He peers intently at one of the brownish photographs. "He really love to take these pictures, Mister Meyers. He save them all. You never see him so happy as when he go into the booths and then get the strip of pictures after—"

I look across the street, toward the school. I anticipate my monkey. "May I keep one?" I ask.

The smile reveals his beautiful yellow teeth. He gives me a strip of four, and, without looking at them, I unzip my briefcase and let them fall inside. "We got lots more. We gone to save them for when we get him out.

Then — " he begins, but stops as the wind rushes through our tunnel again. He rubs furiously at his left eye. I tell him to pull the top eyelid down over the bottom one.

"I be okay," he says. The air is still. "It just a piece of dirt. Only — " He hesitates. "Listen: I only scared on one thing, Mister Meyers, and I telling you the truth." He rolls the top of the grocery bag closed and secures it under his jacket. "That someday I be blind." He stops. "What you think, Mister Meyers?"

I shrug.

"If it happen, I kill myself. That the truth."

"With your eyes," I say, "you will not go blind."

"In Puerto Rico I got two uncles that don't see. Maybe my father too, only we don't know for sure. My brother, Luis, who they got put away now — he got to wear thick glasses — "

"You will not go blind," I say again, and I see him relax. If you cannot see, he says, what's the good? I nod. Though it is too late for other things, this much I can do for him. "You will not go blind."

At once he is out of the shadows, looking from behind the edge of curved bricks, from where I have walked. "I tell you something else, Mister Meyers. With Marty — don't you worry none. After we spring Manuel, I split from him. But for now, I got — " He does not finish the sentence. "¡La jora!" he whispers, and retreats into the shadows. His sneakers, I see, are wet through. "Don't you worry none."

His eyes tell me where to look and I see the policeman crossing the wide street. "He didn't see you," I say.

"You got to get back to work," he says. "I can't take no chances." His hand is on mine. He presses it with his cold fingers. "Maybe when the heat is off — maybe I see you again someday, Mister Meyers — "

I am not sure what I would have done, but there is no opportunity. My monkey is gone, his frail body passing over the snow and slush, his feet dancing across the city's streets. Is that all, I wonder. The policeman glances his way, but does nothing. I look at my open hand and remember his touch. I reach for my briefcase. That is all, I know, and I step out from under the narrow tunnel. I tread through the tire-marked snow. Instinctively my free hand moves to my throat, to my friendly gland. It is there, of course, a gentle reminder. It feels liquid, soft. I know that I would have said nothing to my own monkey. So there was no point in prolonging our meeting.

As I promised, you see, I visited my own doctor on Saturday. He did not agree with the doctor who examined me the night Danny brought me upstairs. That doctor said it was a case of mild shock only. He looked no further. Danny was reassured. My own doctor was more careful. And so there will be no more talk from Harry Meyers about sleeping on his side. I promise you that. There were blood tests, X-rays, some questions, but it was my friendly gland which interested him. Next week he would like me to come into the hospital. Well. It is routine, he assures me, a close look at some of my cells. Perhaps we will remove the entire gland, just to be safe. There were more words, but none of them from Harry Meyers. We know what it all means, after all, don't we?

I am only a block and a half from the school now. Beneath a fire escape I see a sign: *Se necesitan operarios.* Beside me in the gutter, a Puerto Rican family is moving to a new apartment. The wife pushes a baby carriage laden with clothes, dishes, and religious pictures. The husband, a green wool hat pulled over his ears, leans forward against the ice, a rope around his chest, dragging his possessions behind him on a piece of wood. There are roller skates under the wood. Friends of the family surround the cart, keeping the furniture and possessions secure. Behind them come the children, bare-legged, their arms filled with toys. I do not look for particulars. I wish them well also. I have made a decision, you see. I make no predictions about reaching sixty-nine. That was foolishness. I admit it. But if I should not reach sixty-seven, I leave my extra years to you, Ruben Fontanez.

The school blurs in front of me. It must be my glasses. My body aches again. I will miss your eyes, my monkey, but the term has only a few months left. In the cold, the schoolyard is empty. My monkeys will have to eat their government lunches indoors today. I do not hesitate when I am in front of the door. I move swiftly into the building. I do not look at the face of the young school guard who watches the door, and he does not seem interested in me. I smell cigarette smoke but it is nothing to me. NATURE IS ALL AROUND US declares a sign on the first-floor corridor. THE MILKMAN BRINGS US MILK. I do not want to talk to anybody. My chest is heavy and I unbutton my overcoat. I hear the sound of a radio behind me. Mr. Greenfeld, do not come near Harry Meyers today, I warn you. If you are in the teachers' lounge, you had best stay there, do you hear me? THE POLICEMAN IS OUR FRIEND. Do you hear me? I push open a door to staircase "A" and two young people break from their embrace, and flee up the stairs. I would like to tell them to come back. They did not look at me, though. The music on the girl's radio is glorious. I will punch my time card later. If I walk into the main office now there will be too much explaining to do.

At the second floor I do not step into the corridor. I hear the noise of children, shouting in Spanish, cursing their teachers. There are many substitutes today. I wonder what a glance from Mad-Man Meyers would do. There are no pains in my chest though I think I would welcome a pair of them now. I have not changed my mind. If I should not reach sixty-nine I leave my extra years to you, my monkey. I retreat down the stairs and slide along the tiled corridor. I do not look through the windows of classrooms. The auditorium is full. At the front of the room, Mr. Glickman, the ninth grade history teacher, is shouting the names of the thirteen original colonies to his audience. He points to a huge map. He implores his children to repeat the names after him. "Virginia . . . Delaware . . . Massachusetts . . ." Miss Teitlebaum patrols the left aisle and I see the boys' eyes following her chest. In the back row students bend under the seats, stealing puffs of cigarettes. I see a boy's hand under a girl's skirt. She stares ahead, chewing her gum. The movement in the room makes me dizzy. Mr. Glickman gets a group of students to shout back the name of Maryland to him. I hear the muttering in the back rows. What can it all mean to them? A radio blares out a savage beat, and suddenly two students are dancing in the aisle. Mr. Glickman runs toward them demanding that they hand the radio over to him, but it is already making its way from hand to hand, under the seats. The students laugh. He threatens. The buzzer puts an end to the lesson. I back away. The students will fill the corridors momentarily.

I stumble down the hallway, past the main office, down

the few steps, into the street. I look all around me, but I do not think I will see my monkey again, despite his promise. It is much colder now. The sky blackens. I button my overcoat. Sweat pours heavily down my back. I will wait for the classes to change. Then I will try again. Perhaps I cannot begin things anew, but I can return. I see a pair of eyes at the front door window and I step to the side. A moment later Rafael Quinones and one of his young girl friends exit into the snow. He puts two cigarettes in his mouth, one at each corner, and lights them both. His young lady laughs. I see her face. It is Gladys Yambo. She rubs her chest against him, though I do not know what they can feel in such weather. They have not noticed me yet and I cannot understand why. I see Hebrew books tucked under their arms. He pinches her behind and she bites affectionately at his neck. He twists her arm behind her. She screams and her book falls to the ground. I take a step toward them, but Rafael is too quick for me. We are only a few feet apart. Do my eyes deceive me? He has kissed the book. In a perfunctory manner, perhaps, but that does not matter. Their arms around one another they come my way. I press my back against the iron spikes that surround the school and as they dance by they do not notice me. They run across the street. They look back and their eyes move through me. His hand is under her jacket. She stops. Her feet are cold. Well. Yours would be also. I step toward them. There is another buzzer. I lift my briefcase and know that I must prepare myself. Harry Meyers will definitely return. I look across the street but my two children have escaped. I move toward the iron doors. I am listening to you, Ruben Fontanez. Believe me.